Second Chance Holiday

Aurora Rose Reynolds

Copyright © 2014 Crystal Aurora Rose Reynolds Print Edition
Print Edition

Edited by Hot Tree edits Mickey edits, Midian Sosa
Book Cover by Mellissa Gill Designs
Formatted by BB eBooks

Table of Contents

Dedication

Rochelle Paige.

You are an amazing friend, author, and most importantly, mother. Your dedication to your boys is truly inspirational.

Prologue

"**M**IKE?"

I turn around when I hear my name called and come face to face with a beautiful blonde. Her hair is down in waves that reach her shoulders, the top of her head hidden under a bright-pink winter hat. Her creamy, pale skin only causes her bright-blue eyes to look even bigger.

"Mike?" she repeats, searching my face as her cheeks turn pink.

I remember the women I've been with, and she doesn't look familiar. My eyes travel from her face down her body. She's short, her head reaching my chin. The black, thermal shirt and vest she has on show off her full breasts, which lead to a small waist and wide hips. Even with her short height, her legs appear long and are encased in a pair of blue jeans that flare out, showing off a pair of high-heel boots. If by some chance I didn't remember that face, I would definitely remember that body.

"Maybe I'm mistaken. Sorry," she mumbles, ducking her head and walking away.

"I'm Mike," I tell her back as my eyes automatically drop to her ass. Yes, I would definitely remember her.

She turns to face me, and I watch her chest heave as she takes a breath.

"Oh," she says, looking around.

"Do I know you?" I ask, watching as her cheeks darken even more as she looks around the hardware store. *Cute,* I think as I watch her look for an escape.

"Kat. Well, Kathleen Mullings." She shrugs.

Well, shit. I look her over again, but this time, I focus on her eyes—the same eyes I would look into when I was supposed to be studying. Instead, I was wondering what Kat would do if I ever kissed her. We never hung out with the same crowd, but back when we were in high school, I would look for excuses to hang out with her. After graduation, she went away to school and I stayed in Tennessee.

"You're all grown up," I say, watching as a smile spreads across her lips.

"That does tend to happen after thirty-one years." She laughs.

"True." I chuckle and shake my head. "So what brings you to town?"

"I needed a good place to raise my son, so I figured what better place than where I grew up."

"You have a son?" I ask, watching her face light up.

"Yeah. He just turned sixteen."

"Jesus. You really did grow up, didn't you?" I say, covering up the slight disappointment I feel when I think about her having a husband.

"Mom, are you coming or what?"

I look over Kat's shoulder as a tall boy walks down the aisle towards us wearing a hoodie that is pulled up on his head, a pair of baggie jeans, and boots. His eyes come to me and narrow before looking at his mom again.

"Honey, this is Mike. We went to school together. Mike, this is my son, Brandon."

"Nice to meet you." I stick out my hand and he looks at it for a second before giving it a shake.

"Are you ready to go?" he repeats as soon as he drops my hand.

Kat pulls her bag off her shoulder and pulls out her wallet before handing him a twenty and a set of keys. "Go pay for the stuff. I'll meet you at the car," she tells him.

He looks at me again then shakes his head before walking off.

"Sorry about that. He's been like that since the two of us moved here," she says quietly, watching him go. Then her eyes come back to me when I speak.

"No problem." I smile a real smile then feel like an ass for being happy that his dad's not in the picture.

"I need to go, but we should get a drink sometime and catch up."

"Are you asking me out?" I tease.

"No," she says, and her eyes get big when she realizes what she just said.

"Give me your phone." I hold out my hand.

She pulls her phone out of her pocket, handing it to me. I quickly plug my number into her phone before pressing call. When I hear my phone ring, I hang up then pull my phone out and save her number.

"I'll call you."

"Oh, okay." She looks adorably stunned, and the urge to pull her to me and press my mouth to hers hits me in the chest so hard that I have to take a step back.

"See you around, sweetheart," I say, and she blinks then shakes her head. It makes me feel better to know she feels it too.

"Uh…see you around." She turns around.

I watch her walk away. As she reaches the end of the aisle, she looks over her shoulder at me and smiles, giving a wave before turning away again.

"Who's that?"

I spin my head quickly and meet Asher's eyes. "An old friend…" I run my hand over my head then look around, trying to remember what the hell I came in here for to begin with.

"You were giving her the look," he says.

I look at him again and narrow my eyes. "Why are you here and not at home with my daughter and grandbabies?"

"Your daughter's hair keeps clogging up the damn drain," he says, holding up a bottle of Drano. "So me, being the amazing husband I am, told her that I would go to the hardware store then stop off at Annie's and get doughnuts for her 'cause they are her favorite. Now, tell me why you were giving that lady the look."

"There was no look," I deny, looking around again.

"Oh, there was a look," he says, and my eyes go back to him and he smiles.

"Do not say anything to November," I plead immediately.

"Sure." He shrugs.

"Two months ago, she signed me up for a dating website. I do not need help dating," I remind him, and he starts to laugh.

"That shit was funny."

"Funny?" I shake my head and shudder. Some of the replies I received were downright scary.

"She just wants you to be happy."

"I know," I say quietly.

Chapter 1

KAT

I BEND OVER, find my jeans, and quickly pull them on. I find my tank next and pull that on over my head before taking a seat and pulling on my boots. I hate this part; the whole leaving thing really bothers me. It makes me feel dirty, like I've done something wrong. How can something that feels so right be wrong?

Almost a year ago, when I saw Mike for the first time after so many years, I didn't know what to think. The boy who I used to help study had turned into a gorgeous man. He was always good-looking, but after a few years had been added, everything about him held a story, from the small smile wrinkles around his eyes to the calluses on his hands.

I doubt that anyone who met him would think that he was anywhere near his forty-seven years, but he aged well. His height of six feet on the dot would probably not be tall to most, but at five two, I have to tilt my head back to catch his eyes. His dark hair, which was always unruly, still looks the same—long enough that, if you happen to be standing next to him, your hands itch to run your fingers through it. His naturally tan skin, which turns golden after a long summer, always makes his hazel eyes appear more emerald. The tattoos that now cover his arms and chest are something new, but they also tell their own story and change his classic good looks to something more rugged.

I had a crush on him in high school, and the years didn't diminish my feelings. If anything, my crush has seems to have turned into lust, and now, love was mixed in there as well.

The crush I could deal with. It was just an innocent emotion I could easily block out. Lust? That is something completely different. My body craves his touch; I want to be around him and I want him to want me. And now that I've been feeling the love bug, it is no longer just my body that wants him. I want to hear him laugh or talk. I want to share my day with him. But since our first date, we agreed that we're never going to be anything more than what we are now, which is basically fuck buddies.

At forty-three years old, I did not want this to be my life. My son is going to be eighteen in a week, and he's going off to college at the end of the year. I'm not getting any younger, and I want someone to share my life with.

I look at the closed bathroom door, where Mike disappeared to moments ago, and sigh. I know what I need to do, but that doesn't mean I want to do it.

Once I finish putting on my boots, I stand and run my fingers through my hair, trying to tame it. I look at the bed, and my stomach twists. Sex between us is phenomenal. He knows exactly how to touch me, but I desire more. *No, I deserve more.*

I hear the bathroom door open and almost back out of what I need to do. The sight of Mike in nothing but a towel doesn't help at all. I still have no idea how he can have so many muscles at his age, but he does. I close my eyes, take a breath, and open my eyes at the sound of his voice.

"You're leaving?" His eyes come together in confusion.

I know what he's thinking—not that I don't leave after sex, just that we normally spend the entire day together. But after that last round, where the word love was pressed to the roof of my mouth so hard that I wanted to cry, I knew then that I needed to end things between us.

"I can't do this anymore." Okay. The words are out. I can breathe again.

"What do you mean you can't do this anymore?" His eyes narrow further and drop to my hand as I pick up my bag.

"This thing between us… I can't do it anymore." I shake my head, lifting my bag up and over my shoulder.

"This thing?" The words are growled and his eyes sweep the room.

I take a second to think about what I need to say before opening my mouth again. "You were honest with me and told me that you weren't looking for a relationship." I take a breath, feeling my heart speed up. "Nine months ago, I was okay with that because I felt the same way." I smile but feel it wobble. "I no longer feel that way. I want more."

He runs a hand over his hair, and I see pain flash through his eyes. The urge to comfort him hits me hard.

"I told you," he whispers.

He's right. He did tell me what his daughter's mother had done to him, but that was years ago. I don't want to sound like a heartless bitch, but people get screwed over every day. Sometimes, you have to get over shit. My ex-husband abandoned me, and as horrible as that is, I know that not all men are the same and somewhere out there is a man who will love me the way I need to be loved. Even if the man I wanted to love me didn't.

"You did tell me, but I can't be stuck in the past with you, Mike. I don't want to spend the rest of my life alone."

"You're not alone," he says, his eyebrows pulling together. I want to laugh at how oblivious he is.

"Mike, I see you for a few hours a couple of times a week. We have sex. Then I go home. We don't have dinner or talk about our lives, so yes, I'm alone, and in five years, Mike, I don't want to be alone."

I wait to see if he's going to say something, anything that will change the way I feel right now. If he will try to convince me to stay. But he just stands there looking at me. I shake my head in disappointment and turn for the door.

"Wait. We can do dinner," he says.

A laugh so painful that I have to put my hand to my heart bubbles out of my mouth before I can stop it. I don't even turn around to look at him when I reply.

"Mike, dinner isn't going to change how I feel." I'm positive that dinner would just make this whole thing more complicated, and it doesn't need to be any more complicated.

"Will you please stop?" His hand wraps around my elbow as I start to open the front door. My head drops and I turn to face him. "Give me some time."

My throat clogs and tears sting my nose at the pain I hear in his voice.

"I can't. I'm sorry." I shake my head again, pulling my elbow from his grasp before heading out to my car. I don't want things to end like this, but there's no way I can continue with the way things are going.

I quickly buckle up and start my car. I look up at the house one last time. Seeing Mike standing on the front porch makes me question my decision. Then I think about my life and what I want for myself and put my car in reverse, pulling my eyes from him and backing out of his driveway.

I LOOK AT the guy across from me and bite the inside of my cheek. I signed up for online dating three week ago and have gone out on two dates so far. This guy is better-looking than the last guy, but I just mean better-looking, not good-looking.

"I'll be right back," I tell Steve.

He nods, not even taking his eyes off the phone in his hand. I roll my eyes and stand up, grabbing my bag. As soon as I reach the restroom I step up in front of the sink and turn on the cool water, splashing some on my cheeks before looking at myself in the mirror. I told Mike that I didn't want to be alone in five years and I need to date in order for that to happen, so that's what I've been doing.

Mike has called a couple of times, and when he does reach out to me, I can't help but pick up my phone. Call me weak if you want to, but I love him. He never says anything about hooking up again. He just asks how work's going and if Brandon is doing okay. I try to keep the conversations short. My heart can only take so much.

After shaking the thoughts of Mike out of my head and pulling a couple of paper towels out of the dispenser, I dab my face, reminding myself that I just need to get through dinner. Then I can go home, have a glass of wine, and curl up in bed with some twenty-something hot guy with tattoos on my Kindle. I touch up my lip gloss, step out of the bathroom, and run right into a solid wall.

"Sorry," I mumble, as warm hands wrap around my shoulders steadying me. A familiar smell surrounds me as my eyes travel up and meet a pair of warm, hazel eyes.

"Kat." The sound of my name leaving his mouth has goose bumps breaking out across my skin and anxiety turning in my stomach.

"Mike." I try to take a step back, but his hands hold me a little tighter as his eyes travel down my body, taking in my dress and heels.

"You look beautiful," he says as his hands slide down my arms and his thumbs run over my bare skin. My stomach flips at the look in his eyes.

"Thanks." I try to take a step back again, but he leans in, his nose running along my neck.

"You smell good, too."

I take a shaky breath and close my eyes as his nose runs up my neck towards my ear.

"What are you doing here?" he asks, his lips brushing my lobe.

My hands come up to grip his shirt so I don't fall on my face.

"Kathleen, are you okay?" Steve's voice cuts in.

I let go of Mike immediately and take a step away from him. "I'm fine, Steve," I say, taking another step back, trying to get my body back under control.

"Dinner's just arrived at the table and I can't eat until you get there," he says, slightly annoyed.

I look from him to Mike and take a breath when I see the look on Mike's face. "I'm coming now," I tell Steve, who mumbles something before crossing his arms over his chest watching us.

I start down the hall towards him when he clears his throat. If the feeling of guilt weren't running through me for what just happened, I would tell Steve where to shove it. When I reach the end of the hall, I feel eyes boring into my back. I turn my head to look over my shoulder and look at Mike.

"It was nice seeing you," I tell Mike.

He doesn't say anything. He just lifts his chin in my direction before looking over my head and glaring. I turn back around and head out to the dining room, following behind Steve. When we sit at the table, he looks at his food, grumbling under his breath about the temperature before he starts eating. Why the hell I needed to be here in order for him to eat is still confusing me as I start to cut up the ravioli that I ordered.

Suddenly, I feel eyes on me again, so I lift my head. My eyes lock on Mike's from across the restaurant as he sits at the bar with a guy who I know is his brother. His hand, which is holding a beer, comes up in my direction before I lower my eyes to continue eating.

This date will go down as the second worst date of my life, and that's second to the one I had a week ago with a computer programmer who thought he was God's gift to women. Sadly, he reminded me of the aliens from *Men In Black*—the ones with the giant, beefed-up bodies and teeny tiny heads. Yeah, that was not a good time.

"I can't believe that you were making out with someone while we're on a date," Steve says, catching me off guard and bringing me out of my thoughts.

Guilt turns my stomach at his words. My ex-husband cheated on me. He was having an affair for two years and I didn't even find out until he was packing his stuff to move out. I begged him to work it out, but in the end, he chose his new girlfriend and her kids over my son and me. I hate cheaters, and even though I have no commitment to Steve, I still feel guilty for what happened with Mike.

"I wasn't making out with him," I say defensively.

"His mouth was on you." Okay, so that was true. "I would appreciate it if you didn't touch other men when we're out together."

That wouldn't be too hard because I'm thinking this is going to be the last time I will ever see Steve.

"Don't worry. It won't happen again," I tell him, really wanting to stab him.

I sit there for a few more minutes, not eating while feeling holes being drilled into me from across the room. It's taking everything in me not to look at Mike. My body knows he's near. I swear I can feel my blood cells pulling me in his direction.

"I'll be back," I tell Steve.

His eyes narrow, but he nods like I need his damn permission. I grab my bag and start toward the restrooms, but instead of walking all the way down the hall, I turn to the left and head towards the hostess.

"Is everything okay?" the hostess asks as soon as I make it to the front of the restaurant.

"Actually, I need to leave. I have an emergency." I pull out a hundred-dollar bill and hand it to her. "Can you please give that to our waitress and give a message to my date that I left?"

"Sure," she replies, giving me a knowing smile. She seated me with Steve thirty minutes ago, so I'm sure she understands why I want to get out of here.

I smile, lift my bag up over my shoulder, and head for the front of the restaurant. Once I reach the parking lot, I find my keys, quickly get in my car, and take off like the hounds of Hell are on my heels.

When I reach my house, my cell starts ringing from my purse. I pull it out and slide my finger across the screen when I see that Mike is calling.

"That didn't last long," he says, his tone almost playful.

But something about his words pisses me off. I know what I want out of life, and I know that I deserve to have a man who is supportive at my side. I have been single for a long time, but I miss having someone to wake up to or someone to call when I just need to vent.

"He was kind of lame, babe."

"Seriously?" I hiss. My stomach tightens and the urge to throw my phone across the room consumes me. "You're a jerk!" I say, hanging up.

When my phone lights up again, I hit the power button. *Screw him.*

Chapter 2

MIKE

I LOOK AT MY coffee and rub the space between my eyes. I need to get dressed, but since everything went down with Kat, I haven't felt like doing shit. I hear the front door open and slam then the sound of Beast's dog tags jingling together before I ever see November come around the corner.

"Hey, Daddy!" my daughter says, walking into the house.

I watch as she tosses her bag across the room and onto the couch before coming to sit down at the island next to me with a huff. Her eyes search my face for a second before I turn away from her.

"Hey, baby girl," I mumble, taking a drink of my coffee, setting my elbows down on the counter.

"Okay, spill it," she says, raising an eyebrow.

"Spill what?"

"Oh lord. Don't play dumb. You've been moping around for a while and I'm tired of it."

"I'm not moping."

"If you don't tell me what's going on, I'm going to call Grandma," she says, standing and walking around the island into the kitchen. Then she grabs a coffee cup out of the cupboard before pouring herself a cup of coffee.

"Can you drink that right now?" I ask.

She frowns at me over the top of her coffee cup, making me smile. "Ha, ha. Very funny. Now seriously. Tell me what's going on?"

I sigh then debate about what I'm going to tell her. I know she's not a little girl, but the idea of explaining to her how I let the woman I love slip through my fingers because I'm a dumbass is not at all appealing.

"Dad, talk to me," she says quietly.

I look at her across the counter and lower my head. "I fucked up. I mean really fucked up, and I don't know if I can fix it."

"Are you still breathing?" she asks softly, and I lift my head.

"Pardon?"

"Are you still breathing?" she repeats, searching my face.

"Yes," I tell her and frown when I see her eyes flash.

"Do you love her?"

"Yes," I whisper.

She nods. "You know, this man once told me that, as long as you were breathing, anything was possible." She takes a drink of her coffee, searching my face again. She shakes her head and I see tears fill her eyes. "You could have given up on me," she whispers, and my heart contracts. "You could have just said screw it and given up, but you didn't—you never did. You are someone who fights for what you want. So if you love this woman, she's probably pretty amazing and worth fighting for."

"She is," I say, my jaw locking.

"Then fight, Dad. I want you to be happy. You deserve to be happy."

"When did you get so darn smart?"

"I don't know." She shrugs, taking another drink from her cup.

"Love you, baby girl."

"Love you too, Dad." She smiles then leans onto the counter with her elbows. "Now tell me about her."

"What?"

"Who is she?" she asks.

I take a breath and sit up on the stool. "Her name's Kathleen. We knew each other back in school before she moved away," I say.

She nods before taking another drink and then lowering her cup to the counter. "How long have you been seeing each other?"

Shit, I think, and she narrows her eyes.

"How long have you been seeing her, Dad?" she repeats.

"Nine months," I mumble looking down at the counter.

"Nine months? You've been seeing her for nine months and I'm just now hearing about her?" She shakes her head and stands to her full height before turning away from me and walking around the kitchen twice. Then she stops in front of me, opening and closing her mouth again and doing another circle. "I can't believe you haven't told me about this," she says, making me feel instantly worse.

"She has a son."

"She has a son?" she repeats, coming around the counter to sit on the stool next to me again. "How old is he?"

"Just turned eighteen."

"Wow," she breathes.

"Yeah," I say, running my fingers though my hair.

"How do you guys get along?"

"I don't know him."

"You've been seeing this lady for nine months, you're in love with her, and you don't know her son?"

"I told you I fucked up," I tell her, lowering my head towards the counter again.

"You weren't lying," she mumbles under her breath, and I swing my head towards her and narrow my eyes. "It's okay," she says, holding up her hands. "It's not too late." She wraps her arm around my back, laying her head on my shoulder. "You're pretty easy to love, Dad, and one thing I know for sure is that everything will work out."

"You're right, baby girl." I wrap my arm around her, lean in, and kiss the top of her head. And pray that I find away to get my woman back.

Chapter 3

KAT

"**A**RE YOU SURE this is a good idea?" I ask Conner as we pull up in front of a large log house.

"Honey, I told you before. It's all good. We're not going to stay long—just a beer. Then we can go to the movies, or if you want, we can go back to my place," he says, his voice changing slightly, making me panic.

Oh God. I wasn't ready for that. Conner is a very nice man. He's good-looking, attentive, and kind. He's also successful, but the idea of doing anything more than kissing him on the cheek makes me feel nauseated.

I feel bad that there is no spark with him. He has done everything to make me feel comfortable, but something keeps holding me back. There are just no sparks. I keep asking myself, *Who the hell needs sparks?* But my brain is not listening.

I've gone out with Conner a few times. I met him when we were both in line at the bank. He seemed like a nice guy, and I'm still adamant about getting over Mike and finding someone to build something lasting with. Yeah, I know I'm breaking the rules about being an independent woman, but I know what I want. And since the man I want is an idiot, I need to look elsewhere.

"We can go to a movie," I tell him right away and see disappointment flash through his eyes before he takes his eyes off me and looks at the house in front of us.

"Let's go in," he says, opening his door and climbing out of his truck.

I open my door and meet him in front of the house. He takes my hand in his and I fight the urge to make him release me as we walk up the steps to the front porch. When we reach the door, he doesn't knock; he just walks in. The second we step over the threshold, I'm bombarded by the sounds of people laughing and having a good time.

Conner leads us through the crowd, stopping along the way to say hi to people he knows. When we reach the kitchen, a young, very good-looking guy with his hair shaved off comes up to us, pulling Conner in for a one-arm hug. When they pull away, the guy looks at me and then to Conner. Again, something flashes in his eyes, but I'm not fast enough to understand what it is.

"Asher, this is Kathleen. Kathleen, this is Asher."

"Nice to meet you." I smile and take his hand when he puts it out for a shake.

"You look familiar," he says, and I shake my head no. "Do you know my wife November?" he asks.

My stomach drops. No way. Fate cannot be this cruel. But the chance of another woman named November living in this town is about as likely as being struck by lightning. I've never met November, but Mike talked about her often, along with his granddaughters—he even brought up his son-in-law a few times, but I never put two and two together.

I'm an idiot.

"Babe!" Asher yells across the room.

I turn my head in the direction his eyes are facing and see a beautiful woman smile and walk towards us holding a little girl in her arms.

"You called?" she asks, rolling her eyes.

"You know Conner, baby, and this is Kathleen," he tells her.

When she reaches his side, his arm goes around her waist and her eyes come to me. "Kathleen," she mumbles. The look in her eyes is making me wonder if Mike ever told her about me.

"Nice to meet you," I tell her, wanting to break the awkward moment.

Conner's hand goes to my back and my body stiffens at the contact. November's eyes look between Conner and me and a smile starts to spread across her lips.

"Nice to meet you, too," she says then looks down at the girl in her arms. "This is June," she says, lifting the little girl higher up on her hip before stepping out of her husband's grasp.

November pulls me in for a one-arm hug, forcing the little girl in her arms between us. When she starts to pull away, the little girl grabs on to the front of my shirt. I look down at her and smile.

"She's adorable," I say, looking up at November.

June doesn't let up. Instead, she seems to hold on tighter to me as her mom starts to pull her away.

"Can I?" I ask.

November nods, and I take the girl completely from her, pulling in a lungful of her baby smell.

"Your dad around?" I hear Conner ask as I run my fingers down June's chubby cheek.

"Yep. He's manning the grill," Asher tells him.

"I'll be back," Conner says, squeezing my side before walking away.

I feel a singe across my skin and turn my head, looking around the room full of people before locking on Mike. Even from the distance between us, I can see his jaw grinding.

"So you're the one who has my dad all messed up?" November asks.

I pull my eyes from Mike and look at her. "Sorry?"

"My dad," she says, looking behind me. "He's been moping around for a while. He spoke about you to me about a week ago when I threatened to sic Grandma on him if he didn't tell me what was going on."

"I'm sorry," I whisper. This is not what I wanted.

"Don't be," she whispers back, her smile catching me off guard.

I feel a hand at my back and don't even have to turn my head to know that it's Mike.

"You're here with Conner?" is growled near my ear as Asher reaches over, plucking June from my arms, giving me a soft smile before wrapping an arm around November's waist and leading her away.

"Nice to meet you, Kathleen," November calls over her shoulder before looking at her dad and shaking her head.

"Mike, I—" I start to tell him that I'm sorry when he cuts me off.

"No. Actually…" He shakes his head. "Fuck no. You didn't even give me a second to work shit out in my head," he says, his voice low, and my hands begin to shake.

"Don't do this here," I whisper.

"I wouldn't have to do this shit here, but seeing's how you ain't returning my calls, I got no choice."

"Mike."

"Don't Mike me, baby. I'm pissed the fuck off right now."

"You have no right to be mad." I frown.

"No?" He looks at me, top to toe, shaking his head. "I've had my mouth and hands on every inch of you. And you show up at a party at my kid's house with a date." He shakes his head again.

"Don't be a vulgar. And I had no idea this was your daughter's house," I tell him, feeling my face heat in embarrassment.

"You may not have known, but Conner knew this is my daughter's house. As for being vulgar," he says, his face dipping even closer to mine, his voice dropping, "your body knows me, craves me."

"Not anymore," I bite out, becoming pissed off.

"You've been mine since you walked back into my life."

"You tol—"

He cuts me off, ducking his head so he's face to face with me. "I know what I said, baby. I thought that you were cool with how we were. You told me you wanted to keep things simple 'cause your boy. I had no clue that you were feeling like you weren't important to me." His hand comes up, his fingers wrapping around the back of my neck.

"You didn't stop me from leaving," I say quietly, still hurt by that.

"I was caught off guard. I thought I had time. Then I saw you out on a date and was pissed but happy the guy was a loser." He smiles and I narrow my eyes. "Then I called you. I wanted to laugh about it with you, but that's not what happened."

"No," I agree. "I was really mad at you. I *am* really mad at you."

"You think weeks of silent treatment hasn't shown me that?"

My heart starts to feel lighter, and then guilt starts to kick in.

"I'm here with Conner."

"You were here with Conner. Now, you're here with me."

"Mike," I whisper-hiss his name.

"Babe, I'll talk to Conner."

I shake my head. "You're not talking to Conner."

"Did you know Conner knew I was seeing you?"

"What?"

"Every man in town knew I was seeing you. They all knew you were off-limits."

"What?" I repeat, stunned.

"You never wondered why the fuck no one ever hit on you?" he asks, his thumb sliding down my throat.

"No," I answer, swallowing at the intense look in his eyes.

"They knew you were off-limits. Just 'cause our relationship wasn't out in the open doesn't mean I hid that shit."

"Oh my God," I breathe.

"That's why me and Conner are gonna talk," he states, and anxiety fills my chest.

"I'm still mad at you."

"Don't matter. I'm still talking to him."

"Mike."

"Kat."

"Don't be a jerk," I hiss and try to break out of his grasp.

His hand wraps around my waist and his hand at my neck slides farther back into my hair, holding me captive as his mouth comes down on mine, pulling the air from my lungs. I gasp in surprise, and he takes the opportunity to slip his tongue between my lips. His familiar taste fills my mouth, and my body, which is completely owned by him, leans in until my chest is pressed firmly to his. When he groans and I feel his arousal at my stomach, a whimper escapes into his mouth.

"Seriously?" I hear barked.

My eyes squeeze shut. Then Mike's forehead touches mine for a brief second before he pulls away.

"You, me, outside," he tells Conner, jerking his head towards the front door.

My hand covers my mouth and I look around the room at all the people who have stopped to watch what's going on. I can't believe I just kissed Mike in front of all of these people; I really can't believe I did it when I am out with Conner.

"Oh shit. This should be good."

I look to my left at a young guy. His head's shaved. He looks similar to Asher, and I wonder if they're brothers.

His eyes come to me and a smile spreads across his lips. "I'm Trevor."

"Kathleen," I say then hear yelling and start to head towards the front of the house.

"Don't think Mike would want you out there, doll," a guy covered in tattoos says, stepping in front of me.

"I need to stop them."

"Sorry," he says, and I try to step around him, but he blocks my way again.

"Move." I glare, and he smirks, shaking his head.

I look around me and see a sliding glass door not far from where I'm standing. I'm just about to make a run for it when Mike comes storming back into the house carrying my purse, which I left in Conner's truck.

"Let's go," Mike says, and the tattoo guy in front of me smiles before stepping out of the way. When Mike reaches my side, his hand slides around my waist and his eyes go to the tattoo guy.

"Thanks, Nico, and tell November I'll call her," he says before leading me out of the house.

"What are you doing?" I ask when I finally find my voice.

"We're going to my house so we can talk," he says, opening the passenger's side door to his car and pushing me in before slamming the door closed.

"What just happened?" I whisper to myself as I watch Mike slide behind the wheel.

"Seatbelt, babe," he says as I sit there, stunned. His arm comes across me, pulling the belt across my body before locking it in place.

"Mike."

"We'll talk soon," he tells me, starting up the car and putting it in reverse.

"Mike."

"Just a minute, babe," he mutters, pulling out his phone and pressing a couple of buttons before putting it to his ear. "I won't be at the club tonight. Can you handle it?" he asks into the phone while turning his car onto the main road. "Good. Thanks," he mutters before pulling the phone from his ear and putting it in the cup holder between us.

"Can you take me home?" I ask softly.

His hand comes to mine in my lap. He twines his fingers with mine before pulling my hand to his mouth and whispering, "No," against my fingers.

"I just kissed you when I was out on a date with someone else," I tell him.

"I know," he replies, pulling my hand to his thigh.

"I feel really horrible about that, Mike."

"I know that, too."

"I need to apologize to Conner."

"No, you don't," he says firmly.

"Mike, you know about my past, about my ex and what he did to me. I doesn't sit well that I did that to someone else."

"Did you sleep with him?" he asks on a growl.

"What?"

"Did you sleep with Conner?" he repeats, sounding even angrier.

"No," I whisper.

"Do you like him?"

"He was nice."

"Nice?" he says, his face showing disgust.

"Yes. Nice."

"Could you see yourself with him in five years?" he asks, and I turn my head to look at him, noticing that his jaw is clenched.

"No," I say quietly.

"Then you don't need to call him."

We drive the rest of the way to his house in silence. My brain keeps repeating everything that just happened and I have no idea why I'm not fighting him or why I don't have more of an issue with his telling me that I can't call Conner. All I keep thinking about is that, every time he touches or kisses me, it feels right.

When we pull up to his house, he shuts down the car and immediately gets out, walks around to my side, opens my door, leans in across me, unhooks my belt, and pulls me out with him.

"Um," I mumble, not sure what I'm going to say as he shuts the door behind us.

He grabs my hand, dragging me with him into the kitchen. "Sit here," he says as his hands go to my waist, hoisting me up on to the counter. Then he kisses me on the lips before going to the fridge and getting two beers.

I watch him, at a loss for words, while he pops the tops on both beers before coming to stand in front of me, pushing my legs apart, and then standing between them.

"Now, let's talk," he says, setting his beer down at my hip. His hands slide around me, pulling me closer to him. "First, I fucked up, but this is how it's supposed to be. There is supposed to be an *us*."

I can feel my mouth opening and closing, but no words are coming out.

His eyes search my face, his voice drops and his hands go to my face, holding it gently. "I love you. You love me."

I double blink and feel my insides melt.

"I messed up."

What the hell is going on?

I look around the kitchen, making sure that I'm not getting Punk'd. Men do not do this—at least not the men I know. Then again, Mike has never been normal—hence my not being able to get over him.

"Do you forgive me?" he asks softly, his eyes pleading.

I take a deep breath, holding it in. I still can't form words as I look into his eyes. I know we have a lot to work through, but I want to be with him. So I take my hands off the counter, place them on his shoulders, and lean in, pressing my mouth to his. His hands hold my face more firmly while he takes over control of the kiss by tilting my head farther so he can get deeper. His tongue tangles with mine and the feel of his hand skimming down my side to run smoothly over my breast causes me to lift my hips and circle my legs around his waist. Then he pulls his mouth away and rests his forehead against mine with his eyes closed.

"We have a lot to work out," I say softly.

He nods, his hands sliding around me.

"If we're going to do this, I want all of it, not just the sex." I know deep down that I'm just as guilty as he is for what happened between us before. I should have told him sooner that I wanted more before flipping out and jumping ship.

"You got me, Kat."

I search his face and see the truth and love in his eyes.

"You love me too, right?" he asks, sounding worried. "I didn't get that wrong, did I?"

"I do love you," I whisper. This is not what I thought would happen between us.

"So all the rest can be worked out."

"All the rest can be worked out," I repeat as his arms wrap around me and he pulls me into his chest.

"Now, is it time for make-up sex?" he asks with a grin, making me tilt my head back and laugh at the hopeful look on his face.

When I get control of my laughter, I search his face. The look in his eyes makes me pause. He's still smiling, but he looks vulnerable. He's not used to the things he's feeling, and I know that, if we're going to do this right, we need to take it slow for both of us.

"How do you feel about watching a movie and making out with me?" I ask with a smile.

"We can do that," he says softly, helping me off the counter and grabbing our beers before leading me into the living room.

We are just getting comfortable when my phone rings from my bag in the kitchen. I know from the tone that it Brandon. I get up off the couch and go to my bag, pulling out my phone.

"Hey, honey," I answer, putting the phone to my ear.

"Where are you?"

"Excuse me?" I ask, hearing the anger in his voice.

"I heard you were with Mike."

"I am with Mike."

"Mom, what the fuck?"

"Brandon, you're the child. I'm the parent," I remind him. Since we have been on our own without his dad, he has been stepping over his boundaries more and more.

"Whatever," he says before hanging up on me.

I pull the phone away from my ear and look at the screen.

"Everything okay?" Mike asks, making me jump.

I sigh and turn to look at him. As much as I want to hang out, I need to go home and talk to my son.

"I need to go home," I tell him, shaking my head.

"Brandon okay?" he asks, looking concerned.

"Yeah. I just need to go home and have a talk with him."

"I'll drive you."

"Thank you," I whisper, getting my bag and following him out to his truck.

Chapter 4

KAT

I ANSWER MY phone, my voice cracking. "Hello."

"What's wrong, baby?" Mike asks, his voice softening as my body collapses back onto the bed.

"I'm sick," I tell him, pulling the covers over me.

"Where's Brandon?"

"He's staying the night at a friend's house tonight," I mumble, cuddling deeper into my pillow. I woke up with a headache, and throughout the day, I have slowly gotten worse. My nose started running, and then I started getting chills. "I took some medicine," I say absently.

"I'll be over in an hour." His concern comes to me though the phone like a soothing caress.

"You don't need to come," I say immediately, not wanting him to get sick. Working from home, I'm able to make my own schedule, but I know he doesn't have the option of being sick. His club is very important to him and his brother.

"Do you like chicken noodle soup?" he asks, ignoring me and my protest.

"I don't want you to get sick."

"I'll be fine. Now answer my question."

I smile at his bossiness and nod into my pillow as I tell him, "Yes."

"I'll see you soon, baby," he says, softly making my heart swell. Since we got back together, he has been all in and our relationship couldn't be any better.

"'Kay," I whisper, falling asleep.

"Kat, wake up, baby," I hear then feel a cool rag on my forehead.

I open my eyes slowly. They feel so heavy.

"Hey," Mike says, running a finger down the underside of my jaw. "I need you to sit up and take some medicine for me."

I blink and slowly sit up with his help. "Thanks," I tell him, taking the pills from his hand and putting them in my mouth before taking the cup from him and swallowing them down.

"You got a thermometer?"

"In the bathroom," I whisper.

He gets up and leaves, coming back a few seconds later with it in his hand. "Open up, babe," he says, sitting on the side of the bed near my hip.

I open my mouth before closing my lips around it. When I hear it go off, I open my eyes, not even having realized they were closed.

He removes it from my mouth and shakes his head. "One-oh-two," he says, looking at me worriedly.

"I'll be okay." I lean my head against the headboard and pull the covers up to my waist.

His hand comes up, his fingers running along my hairline. "I'd feel better if you didn't have a temp."

I smile. "You can't control everything."

"I don't like you sick. How about you take a shower while I

make you some soup?"

"Okay," I sigh. I can tell by the look on his face that he's not going to give up until my temperature is down. I sit up completely, and he helps me into the bathroom, starting the shower for me before helping me remove my clothes. There is nothing sexual about it, and I can tell by the concentration on his face that he is just focused on taking care of me and helping me get better.

"You gonna be okay or do you want me to stay in here?" he asks, helping me into the shower.

"I'll be okay." I nod, tilting my head back under the water.

The feel of the warm water running over me makes me sigh in relief. I open my eyes when I don't hear him say anything else. His hands are above his head, holding on to the shower rod, the muscles of his harms flexing. The look on his face has me swallowing hard.

"I was good until you made that sound," he says, his voice raising the hairs on my arms.

"What sound?" I ask. Even though I'm sick, I feel my body react to the look in his eyes.

"It's this noise you make when I slide inside you. I haven't heard it in so long. When the sound left your mouth, my boy woke up," he says, tilting his head down toward his crotch.

I lower my eyes and see the large outline of his erection through his jeans. We haven't had sex since we got back together. Between Brandon, work, and Mike's schedule at the club, we haven't been able to spend more than a few hours together. Now, after not having had him for so long, my body is waking back up. It never took much for him to get to me. I swear I can feel myself get wet just by thinking of him.

"I'm gonna go make your soup," he growls.

I nod, licking my lips, my eyes tracking his movements. I want to lean out of the shower and wrap myself around him.

"Motherfucker," he mumbles before turning and leaving me standing in the shower.

I hear him as he goes down the stairs and listen as cabinets open and close. I can't help it; the smile that spreads across my lips gets bigger the louder he becomes downstairs. I can imagine him muttering under his breath while slamming the cabinets.

I finish washing up then get out. I twist my hair in a towel before wrapping up in my favorite robe and climbing back into bed. I turn on the TV just as Mike walks into the room carrying a tray I didn't even know I owned.

"Where did you find that?" I ask him as he walks around the bed, setting the tray down on my lap.

"Brought it with me." He smiles. "Ma was over at my place when I called you. She told me what you would need."

My heart flutters. No one has ever looked after me when I was sick before—not even my ex-husband. He was always too busy. Of course, later I learned that it was difficult for him to be married to me while carrying on a relationship with his girlfriend and her children.

"Thank you," I whisper, looking down at the tray. Not only did he bring me soup, but he also brought me crackers and ginger ale. I dip the spoon into the soup, coming up with broth and tiny stars. I smile bigger as I swallow a spoonful.

"You feel better after your shower?"

"Actually, yes." I nod, watching as he takes off his boots and pulls his shirt off over his head. I don't think I will ever get over the sight of him.

I've never had any problems with my weight. My whole life, I have been the same size. Even when I was pregnant with my son, I didn't gain more than twenty pounds. But Mike's body is something different altogether. His muscles are defined. You can tell just by looking at him that he takes care of himself.

After he is down to his boxers and his clothes are neatly placed in the large, oversized chair in the corner of my room, he climbs into bed next to me, careful not to spill my soup as he wraps an arm around my shoulder.

"You got the remote?" he asks.

Without thinking, I hand it to him. Then he turns on a football game and kisses the side of my head. The whole thing feels surreal. It feels like we have done this a million times.

"What time do you have to go into work?" I ask him. I don't want him to leave, but he works nights and being the owner of a strip club doesn't come with a normal schedule.

"Joe's got it covered tonight," he says absently, his eyes focused on the game.

My insides are turning liquid. He is having his brother take over so he can be with me.

"I'll be okay if you need to go to work," I tell him, scooping up another spoonful of soup.

"He's got it, babe," he says, looking over at me. "The club's not going anywhere. It's probably gonna be a slow night anyway, and Joe can handle it."

"Okay," I whisper.

"Eat," he says, his tone gentle.

I nod and finish eating. When I'm done, he takes the tray downstairs only to come back up carrying a plastic shopping bag. When he gets back into the bed, he dumps the bag out and I start to laugh. There is every kind of medication you could think of, from stuff for colds, period pain relievers, and stuff for gas and bloating.

"I didn't want to have to leave after I got here, so I got a little bit of everything."

"I can see that." I smile then start putting stuff back. "I don't need any of this," I tell him, handing him the bag.

He takes it and puts it on the floor. I pick up the Nyquil and he takes it from me, opening it and pouring it into the little cup before handing the cup to me. I take it immediately before handing him the empty cup back. He puts the stuff on the table next to him before lying down, pulling me with him.

"Thank you for coming and taking care of me."

His hands wrap around me tighter and his lips touch the top of my head. "It's my job to take care of you," he tells me, and I can hear the seriousness in his tone.

"And I get to take care of you."

His body stills and he takes a deep breath. "I'd like that," he says quietly.

I know about his dating history, and I know that he never wanted to get close to anyone again. However, I also know that, even if he told himself that all of his previous bed partners were long term and that he might not have been looking for love, he was not sleeping with a different woman every night. He wanted to connect with someone, but somehow, he never did.

I burrow deeper into his side and angle my face towards the TV.

"Night," Mike says, his lips resting on my forehead briefly before pulling away.

"Night," I whisper back. My eyes close completely, and my only thought is that this is the thing I've been looking for.

"What the fuck are you doing here?" I hear Brandon say.

I sit up quickly, looking at the open door of my room. My eyes meet my son's angry ones. Then his go back to Mike, who is now sitting up as well, wrapping an arm around me.

"Brandon Tim, watch your mouth," I tell him, running a hand through my hair.

"Seriously, Mom, this is bullshit."

"Mind your mom," Mike says in a tone I've never heard from him before.

Brandon glares at Mike then looks at me. "I'm taking the car," he states, his jaw clenching.

I start to nod when Mike cuts in. "Ask."

"What?" Brandon asks, confused.

I hate to admit it, but since my husband left, I have let Brandon do his own thing. I know it's stupid, but I hate fighting with him. I feel so guilty that he no longer has his father in his life, and sometimes, it's just easier to go with the flow than to go head-to-head with an eighteen-year-old man-child.

"Ask if you can use your mom's car. Don't tell her you're taking it," Mike says, not taking his eyes off Brandon.

Brandon's jaw starts to grind and his eyes cut to me. "Can I use the car?" he grits out.

"Yes," I say.

Brandon immediately stomps off down the stairs, slamming the front door behind him, and I flop back on the bed and cover my face.

"Babe."

I just shake my head.

"He knows we're together," Mike says, and I know he knows, but it's one thing to know and another to find your mom in bed with a man.

"I know, but maybe we shouldn't have sleepovers anymore," I say through my hands. I feel the bed move. Then my hands are being pried away from my face.

"First, I came over on a night when he was sleeping at a friend's so that I could take care of you while you were sick," he says softly, pushing my hair away from my face. "That being said, I have a feeling it wouldn't matter if he came home from college and found me in your bed. He would still be pissed off."

"I know," I whisper, feeling tears fill my eyes.

Mike's eyes go soft as he wipes my tears away with his thumbs. "He loves you, baby."

"I know," I repeat on a sob.

He rolls to his side pulling me with him. "What time does he normally get home?" he asks, and I try to bury my face deeper into his chest, not wanting to answer that. "Kat?"

I take a shaky breath before tilting my head back and looking at him. "I told him his curfew is ten on school nights and twelve on weekends."

"Lemme guess. He doesn't come home when he's supposed to?"

"Sometimes." I shrug.

"Babe, I understand that you're trying to soften things up for him 'cause his dad left, but I think you're hurting more than you're helping at this point."

"You don't understand." I close my eyes, shaking my head. My son is so angry. He's a good kid and I know that he loves me, but he has so much anger inside him that I can feel it when we're in the same room.

"I do understand. I know how much trouble teenage boys can

get into when left to do their own thing."

"Mike."

"He's not my kid and I can't tell you what to do or how to raise him, but he needs to have structure and discipline. He's not too old for you to get on him."

"I know," I say because I do know. "I just don't think he was expecting to see you here."

"You told him we're together, right?"

"Yes," I say immediately. "He stormed off, but I didn't think anything of it 'cause he always storms off when I try to talk to him."

"We'll figure it out together," he says, and my heart settles a little bit more. "How are you feeling?" he asks after a few minutes. His hand goes to my forehead and his eyes look me over.

"I feel a lot better."

"Doesn't feel like you have a temp anymore. That's a good thing."

"I actually feel really great. I haven't slept that good in a long time."

"Me neither." He kisses me then pulls away before sitting on the side of the bed and raising his arms above his head.

I watch, fascinated, as his back muscles bunch and expand.

"How about a shower then breakfast?" he asks, looking over his shoulder at me.

I lick my bottom lip and nod when his eyes darken slightly. He stands to come around to my side of the bed. I lie back as his upper body cages me. One hand goes to my hair while the other makes a fist in the bed near my head as his face lowers toward mine.

"How much better are you feeling, exactly?" he asks, his nose running along mine.

"Much better." I put my hands to his chest. Even while lying down, I feel like I need to steady myself.

"Hmmm," he rumbles, his hand in the bed going under me then traveling down my ass to the back of my thigh.

When I feel his hand on my bare skin, I squirm. When his hand travels farther up and his hand grabs on to my bare ass cheek, I bite my lip.

"You don't have on anything under your robe?"

I shake my head no and his eyes turn even darker as they travel down my body, landing on the tie of the robe.

Chapter 5

MIKE

I CAN'T IMAGINE not having this, not having *her*. My eyes skim down her body to the robe, which is tied around her.

Last night, when Kat was in the shower, it almost killed me to go downstairs knowing that she was naked and soaking wet a few feet from me. I haven't even jerked off since she told me that she wanted more and left me stunned, still in my towel, at my house while I watched her drive off. I had known that I love her before she broke down, but I hadn't realized the extent of it or how much she had consumed me.

The night I saw her at the restaurant on her date, I was talking to Joe about her and working out with him what I needed to do. Things were not cut-and-dry. She has a teenage son. I didn't know why that scared me more than anything else. I love kids, but he is not a kid. Brandon is practically a man.

I also had my own baggage, things I needed to deal with. It pisses me off how much November's mother affected me, but she did. The things she did while she was pregnant and then when she took off with my kid have made me question every woman I've come into contact with. Was it fair to loop all women into the category of lying, conniving bitches? No, but it is what it is. Now,

I have a woman who has been honest to a fault since day one under me and I am going to find a way to deal with my insecurities so that we can have a future together.

"You look like you're running a fever," I tell her, untying her robe.

She wiggles under me until her leg comes up to rest behind my thigh so she can pull me closer. I feel the heat of her pussy through the thin cotton of my boxers and groan, pulling her closer to me as I spread the robe open. My eyes travel down her body. She is really beautiful; everything about her appeals to me.

My head lowers and I kiss her, pulling her bottom lip into my mouth before releasing it, my mouth traveling down her jaw, to her neck, then down to her breast. I look up at her, our eyes meeting, as I pull one nipple into my mouth. I suck deep, and her whimper fills the room as I release it and kiss my way to her other breast. I pull it into my mouth, watching her eyes close and her back arch. *Fuck, she's perfect.*

Her legs pull me tighter, and I know what she wants. I pull down my boxers with one hand and wrap my hand around myself before running the head from her entrance to her clit then back down again. I place one last kiss on each nipple before leaning back to look at her.

"Mike."

The sound of my name leaving her mouth is enough to cause my balls to draw up. I watch as I enter her slowly, fighting myself against slamming into her. Her body lifts forward, her hands going to my ass, her nails digging into my skin.

"Fuck. So fucking tight," I groan, pulling out, feeling her muscles clamping down on me and try to pull me back in. "I missed this." I lean over her completely. My feet are planted on the floor, her legs now wrapped around my hips.

"Me too," she whispers, pulling my mouth down to hers.

I push my tongue into her mouth while one hand travels down to wrap around her hip, my thumb sliding over her clit. Her body bucks under me as her moans fill my mouth. I know I won't be able to hold out much longer. I haven't had this in so long and her slick, tight heat is only making it that much harder to hold back.

"So close," she breathes. Her hands move to her breasts, her fingers pulling hard on her nipples.

I lean back, pull her hips up higher, and start slamming into her hard. Her lower body is off the bed, only her shoulders left on the mattress. Looking down her body at my cock sliding in and out of her and at her tits bouncing with each thrust causes my balls to pull up tighter.

"So wet. You feel like silk, so smooth and hot wrapped around my cock." Her lust-filled eyes meet mine and I can feel her get tighter around me. "You're gonna come, Kitten."

She nods, her teeth biting into her bottom lip. I lift my foot up onto the bed and spread her legs wider, pounding into her harder. Her cry and the convulsing of her pussy send me over. I plant myself deep and come hard. My head falls forward, my chest moving quickly. I lift my leg that has fallen asleep and lean forward, sliding my hands under her before pulling her up and then falling to my back with her on my chest without falling out of her.

"You okay?" I ask after I get my breath back.

She nods against my chest, not saying anything.

"We need to shower," I mumble, running my hands down her back.

When she nods again, I feel her cheek move against my chest and I know she's smiling.

"You speechless?"

She nods again, and I laugh.

"You called me Kitten." She giggles, making me smile.

"You don't like it?"

"I do," she whispers then lifts her head to look at me. Her eyes search my face for a long moment before she looks away and lays her head back on my chest.

"What was that?"

"Just happy," she says on a squeeze.

I kiss the top of her head. "You ready to shower?"

"Yeah." She nods, pressing a kiss to my chest before lifting her hips and pushing off the bed.

I watch her walk to the bathroom, mesmerized by the flare of her hips.

"Are you coming?" she asks over her shoulder.

My eyes travel up her body to her face and I smile, getting off the bed following her into the shower.

"I NEED YOU to come down to the station," James says as soon as I pick up the phone.

I look at the clock and see that it's after two in the morning. I know Kat's at home. I talked to her at twelve. She was working on edits for a client. Then was going to get ready to go to bed.

"What's going on?" I ask, grabbing my keys from the drawer. A couple of the girls who worked here would call if they'd gotten in trouble, so it wasn't the first time I have been called away from work to help someone out.

"Brandon was just brought in for drinking."

Shit. I look at the ceiling and pray for patience.

"Is Kat there?" I ask immediately.

Brandon's a good kid with a lot of anger he doesn't know what to do with, so he continues to act out without thinking about the consequences. It doesn't help that his dad is a piece of shit, forcing everything on Kat. My woman is strong, but at the end of the day, the kid needs his dad.

"No. He said he didn't want to call her, and since he isn't a minor anymore, my hands are tied."

"Fuck. Okay. I'm on my way," I tell him before hanging up. When I make it to the front of the club, I find my brother sitting at the bar, going over an order list. "I need to go."

"Everything okay?" he asks, standing and following me out of the club.

"Brandon's at the station with James," I tell him.

His eyes change from curious to concern. "Wha'd he do?"

"He was drunk." I shake my head, unlocking my car.

"You want me to call Kathleen?" Joe asks.

I pause, thinking about it before answering. "No. I'll see her when I drop him at home," I tell him, getting in the car.

"Call if you need me," he says, stepping away from the car.

"Will do," I mumble, slamming the door closed.

I do not want to be in the middle of this, but Kat has been dealing with her son on her own for too long and the kid has been pushing her around, using what happened with his dad as an excuse to be a pain in the ass. So if he wants to call me thinking that, as his mom's man, I'm gonna ease the blow 'cause I wanna be on his good side, he has another thing coming.

By the time I get to the precinct, I'm pissed. When I walk into the building, I can hear someone singing "Call Me Maybe" in a loud tone. I know right away that it's Brandon, and I immediately wonder how much he's had to drink and if he was driving drunk. I walk down into the bullpen and see James talking to another officer.

"Mike," James says as soon as he spots me.

"What exactly happened?" I ask, 'cause if this kid was driving drunk, he is going to learn a hard lesson. His ass will be staying in jail at least until morning—if not longer.

"Him and a couple other boys were drinking in the parking lot of the high school." He looks across the station when the singing stops and the sound of someone getting sick can be heard. "When Braxton pulled up, the other boys ran off. Brandon stayed put and cooperated." He pauses again when the sound of singing picks up once again. "I don't know this kid well, but from what people say, he's a good boy." His arms cross over his chest and his hip leans against his desk.

"He's not a bad kid. He's angry and acting out but not a bad kid," I confirm.

"Braxton told me that he stopped Brandon a week ago for driving recklessly."

"Does Kathleen know about that?" I ask, She never mentioned it to me and I couldn't picture her not mentioning it at least in passing.

"Braxton let him off with a warning." James shakes his head. "Brandon told him that he was just messing around. He didn't have anyone in the car with him and he was in a deserted parking lot, so no one was in any danger. But when he picked him up tonight, he knew that he needed to bring him in."

"Shit," I mumbled, rubbing the back of my neck.

"He was rambling about his dad earlier."

"His dad's a piece of work." I sigh and sit down in one of the chairs, dropping my head towards my lap.

"I think you need to step in. He needs a role model in his life," James says.

I lift my eyes to his. "I own a strip club. I can't exactly take him there to hang out."

"What teenage boy doesn't like women?" James asks, looking at me with a smile twitching his lips.

Braxton laughs.

"I don't know if I'm a good role model." I've never thought about how my owning a strip club would affect any relationship I had. Luckily for me, Kat doesn't have a problem with what I do, but that doesn't mean I think it is a normal occupation for someone with a family.

"You're there. Your club's clean. I'm not saying that he needs to be there. Honestly, I just think he needs something he needs a man in his life that he can look up to."

"I'm not sure my woman would approve of me taking her kid to the strip club."

"You dating his mom?" James asks with a tilt of his head, making me notice for the first time how much his boys take after him.

"Yeah."

"You serious about her?"

"You know I am."

"Then I think you need to figure out how to be what this kid needs so you can be the man your woman needs as well. I've seen it happen too many times. Young man, no one to turn to, starts acting out, ends up in trouble that he can't get out of. I don't want that for you or Kathleen."

I let his words sink in and know I need to do something. I just need to figure out exactly what my role would be.

"I'll figure it out," I tell him.

"Figured you would," James mumbles, taking his eyes off me and looking over at Braxton. "You wanna bring him out?" he asks.

"Yeah," Braxton says, getting up from behind the desk and heading towards the back of the station.

A minute later, Brandon stumbles around the corner with Braxton and I shake my head.

"Mike, Mike, Mike, Mike, Mike, what day is it?" Brandon says as soon as our eyes meet.

"Let's go," I say, ignoring him and grabbing his arm.

"How can someone who owns a strip club be so lame?" he asks, leaning his weight against me.

"You want me to help you get him into your car?" James asks, holding open the door to the station.

"We're good. I'll call you later. We need to figure out when we're doing our fishing trip."

"I wanna go on a fishing trip," Brandon mutters as I lead him out to my car.

"You do?" I ask, surprised. I haven't even thought about taking him because he has never seemed like he wants to even be in the same room I'm in let alone to go away for a few days on a trip.

"My dad was supposed to take me on a trip for graduation, but he told me we can't go 'cause his new kid needs braces," he says and his eyes draw together like he's trying to remember something. "My dad's a piece of shit," he slurs out.

"Your right about that," I mutter in agreement while helping him into my car.

Once I see that he's buckled in, I shut his door, walk around to the driver's side door, and open it.

"We may have to schedule the fishing trip sooner rather than later!" I yell over the roof of my car at James, who is standing in the door of the station.

His eyes go from me to the passenger's side of my car and he nods.

I get in and slam the door. Hearing Brandon talk about his father makes me realize what he has been missing. I have a good dad. Even when he and my mother split, I knew I could depend on him. I don't know what it's like to be a young man without a father to depend on. And it pisses me off that this kid wants to have a relationship with his dad and his father is too blind to understand that he's lucky enough to have the opportunity to know his son, to watch him grow, to help shape the type of man he'll be.

"My mom loves you," Brandon mumbles, rolling his head against the headrest to look at me. "You hurt her, I'll kill you," he says as I pull out onto the highway towards home.

A smile twitches my lips, and I nod before answering. "I love her too, and I won't hurt her."

"Good," he mutters before rolling down the window, sticking his head outside, and getting sick all over the side of my car.

"You're washing my car tomorrow," I tell him, trying not to laugh as he gags harder.

This scenario is familiar. I remember calling my mom to come pick me up when I had drunk too much in high school. The next day, I had to wash the inside and outside of my mom's car. She told me that it was part of my punishment and it worked. I learned my limit quickly.

As soon as we pull up in front of Kat's house, Brandon opens his door and falls out of the car onto the street. I get out, walk around to his side, and help him untangle his foot from where it somehow got stuck on the seatbelt before assisting him to his feet.

"You're a good guy, Mike," he says, patting my chest as he leans into me.

"When you're not drunk, we're gonna sit down and have a talk," I tell him, walking up to the front door and pulling out my key.

"Fuck, you have a key. It is serious," he says, his body almost pulling me down with him.

As I unlock the door and push it open, he leans over and vomits all over the porch. I hold him up, trying to help him over to the grass. The poor kid is going to have one hell of a hangover tomorrow, and cleaning up puke isn't going to help.

"Mike? Brandon?"

I turn slightly to look at Kat, who is standing in the doorway wearing nothing but a robe.

"What's going on? Oh my God. Is he drunk?" she asks, starting to step outside.

I turn towards her, taking one hand off Brandon, placing it in her stomach, and pushing her back inside. "He got sick out here, baby," I tell her, and she nods, looking at her son.

"I thought that, when we moved, you wouldn't do this anymore, Brandon," she says.

I can see the worry in her eyes, and I understand it, but I also understand why her son is acting out right now. Brandon stands up and leans his body weight completely on me.

"Let's get him into bed. Tomorrow, we're all gonna sit down and have a talk," I tell her.

She looks ever more worried. The urge to comfort her almost strangles me, but I need to deal with her son first. Then I can talk to her and hopefully make her understand what's going on and what this kid really needs. She can't continue to act like his behavior is normal. It's not fair to her son or her. Without saying anything else, I follow her into the house and up the stairs towards Brandon's room.

"You want to shower or you want to sleep?" I ask Brandon, who is now moving more quickly to his room.

He lifts his head slightly and looks at me. "I just want to sleep," he mutters, falling back onto his bed.

I find his garbage can and put it next to him. Then I make sure that he's on his side before I pull his shoes off and cover him up. Kat comes in with a cup full of green liquid and holds it to his mouth. He rinses his mouth then leans over to spit in the trash can before lying back again.

"I love you, Mom," he says, closing his eyes.

Kat sits down next to him on the bed, pushing his hair away from his forehead and pressing a kiss there, muttering, "I know you do," softly before pulling away.

"I'm sorry," he says.

I see her body sag. I step towards her, putting a hand to her back.

"This is not okay, Brandon. I love you more than life, but this is not okay." The pain in her voice is obvious and I know she's close to tears.

Brandon's eyes open and he looks at his mom. The look in his eyes is so bleak that I want to track down his father and kill him for doing that to his son and the woman he was supposed to love.

"I'm sorry," he repeats, and I don't even know if he knows

what he's apologizing for.

"We'll talk tomorrow. I'm going to leave your door open so I can hear you if you need me," she tells him, leaning in again and kissing is forehead.

We both head out of his room then down the stairs. I pull off my jacket and toss it onto one of the chairs in the living room before going to the kitchen and grabbing a beer.

Chapter 6

MIKE

"SO WHAT HAPPENED?" Kat asks.

I turn to face her and see that she has her arms wrapped around her waist and her eyes have become full of worry. "James called me and told me that Brandon asked him to call me to come pick him up after he was arrested."

"Why didn't he call me?"

"I think he was hoping that he wouldn't get in trouble if he called me."

"What?" she whispers.

"Baby," I say softly, running a finger down her cheek. "I'm your boyfriend. My guess is he thought I would pick him up and ease the blow with you to try and get on his good side."

"He used to do this before we moved. This was one of the reasons we moved to begin with. He was always hanging out with the wrong crowd. He would come home late or not at all. Sometimes, he would show up drunk or high. I tried to talk to him, but nothing was working. Then I decided to move here. I loved growing up here and figured that it was probably a safe place to raise my son."

She takes a deep breath, letting her hands drop to her side.

"When we first moved into town, he was okay. He was doing good in school and not giving me any problems. Then, a few months ago, right after his birthday, something happened and he stopped listening. He started getting angry easier and our relationship, which had started to repair, went downhill fast." She looks away when I see tears begin to fill her eyes. "I don't know what's going on with him. I don't understand why he's so angry. I don't know why he's mad at me or how to help him."

"I think that whatever happened has to do with his dad more than it has to do with you," I say, and her eyes come back to me. "Did you know that his dad told him that he couldn't take him on a graduation trip because his girlfriend's kid needs braces?" I ask, watching her body still and her face contort with anger.

"No, I didn't know that."

"He did."

"That dick."

"Yep." I nod and take a drink from my beer. "I talked to James, and what he said along with what Brandon said got me thinking," I say, pulling her into me by the rope of her robe. "I think that Brandon needs some male bonding time. Every year, me and the Mayson's go out on the lake for a few days, and I'm gonna take Brandon."

"Really?" she whispers, leaning into me. Her eyes go soft, and I lean in and press my mouth to hers.

"I think it would be good for him and I to get to know each other better. I also think it would be good for him to have someone to look up to. Asher, Trevor, Cash, and Nico are not too much older than him. I know that I don't have a conventional job and I'm not much of a role model, but I think that the other guys will be a good influence."

"You know, when I first found out that you owned a strip club, I was a little put off," she says.

I raise an eyebrow because *a little put off* is a huge understatement.

"Okay, so I was a lot put off," she says, smiling. "But now I know to you. It's your business and nothing more. You would also be a good influence on him. You're a hard worker, you love your child and grandchildren, and you take care of the people you care about. I think all of those things are the qualities of a good man."

My stomach tightens 'cause those are not things I would have thought of. I know that a lot of people look at me and my club and say that I'm taking advantage of the women who work for me and I only see women as sex objects, but in my club, the women are safe. They are treated with respect. Most of them are students or mothers just trying to make a better life for themselves or their families. If I knew that the women who worked for me would be able to find somewhere else to work that had the same kind of environment, I would have closed the doors to Teasers after November moved home.

"Do you think that I should call his dad and tell him that his son needs him?" she asks, bringing me back to the moment.

"I don't need him," Brandon says, swaying into the kitchen. "He has never wanted to be a part of my life—even when you were married to him. He didn't want to be a dad to me, so I don't need him or want him in my life."

"Honey."

"No, Mom. Fuck him," he growls, opening the door to the fridge.

"Watch your mouth," I say.

Brandon looks at me over his shoulder. "You're not my dad,"

he states, holding my eyes.

Mine narrow on him. "You're right. If I was your father, your ass would be handed to you for the stress you're putting your mom through. I'm not your dad, but I'm an adult."

"Whatever," he mutters.

"You feelin' better?" I ask him.

He shrugs, which only pisses me off further.

"You're up and you don't seem as drunk as you were, so take the hose and go wash off my car."

"What?" he asks, looking from me to his mom.

"Go rinse off the vomit from the side of my car."

"But it's, like, midnight or something."

"And?" I ask.

"Mom?" he says, looking at his mom again.

"Don't look at me for help. And when you come in, we need to talk about your punishment."

"Fine," he says, stomping out of the kitchen, the sound of the door slamming shut echoing through the house.

"That went well," Kat says then looks at me and smiles.

"Why are you smiling?"

"My son doesn't agree to do stuff he doesn't want to do. You have to understand that, as much as he's mad right now, he respects you enough to go outside in the middle of the night to clean off your car because you told him to do it. That's huge."

"I think you're reading to much into that, baby."

She shrugs and takes the beer from my hand before putting it to her mouth and taking a drink. "Regardless, thank you for picking him up tonight."

"You're welcome," I tell her, kissing her head.

After about fifteen minutes, the front door opens then shuts and Brandon comes into the kitchen.

"How long am I grounded for?" he asks his mom, and an idea comes to me.

"You're gonna come work for me," I say.

Kat and Brandon both say, "What?" at the same time.

"November has been trying to transfer all the stuff from my office to her home office. You're gonna help her get everything organized."

"So, I'm going to work at a strip club?" he asks.

Kat's mouth has opened and closed a few times, but she still hasn't said anything.

I look from her to Brandon and shake my head. "No, you're not working at the strip club. You're going to help November."

"I think we should talk about this," Kat says.

My eyes go to her and then back to Brandon. When Brandon's eyes come back to me, something flashes in them before he looks at his mom.

"I wanted to get a job anyways, so I think this would be a good opportunity for me," he tells his mom.

I give Kat's waist a squeeze then look at Brandon. He needs something, and though I may not be the best person to give him what he needs, I want him to be successful and I want to heal the rift between him and his mom. *I just hope I don't make shit worse.*

"Okay, but you're still grounded. You can use the car for school and work, but no hanging out with friends for a month."

"A month?" he asks, stunned. Then he looks at me like I should help him out.

"Do I need to remind you that you were picked up by the cops for underage drinking? If you were anyone else, you would have spent the night in jail and had to go in front of the judge in the morning. You're lucky that this is your punishment," I tell him.

Kat leans slightly back into me. "A month, Brandon. If you mess up during the month, another month gets added," she says.

Brandon looks at her and nods.

"I love you, honey. I know that you're mad about your dad and what happened, but I love you and I want you to be a better man than he is, and right now I'm worried about you," Kat says softly.

Brandon's body loosens completely. He nods again, and Kat steps out of my hold and gives him a hug.

"WANT A BEER?" Asher asks.

Brandon's face lights up and his hand goes forward to take the beer when Nico snatches the beer from Asher and opens it.

"Sorry, kid. You need to get some hair on your chest. Then you can have a beer," Trevor says, handing Brandon a soda, smirking.

"Whatever," Brandon grumbles, sitting back in his chair and taking a drink of his soda before looking around the campsite.

It's been over a month since I picked up Brandon from the station. He has made a lot of changes since then. He is home more often than not or he is hanging out with me, Joe, or one of the Maysons. His grades have improved, and his and Kat's relationship has done a complete one-eighty. Not only has he been helping November, but he has also shown a great interest in the club and improving it. I know nothing about social media, but the kid is a damn wiz and he has helped build clientele online with Twitter, Facebook, and Instagram. Joe is completely impressed with the damn kid, and I have to say I'm proud as hell of him.

"So, who is the girl you were hanging around the other day?" Nico asks.

I look at Brandon and then Nico and raise an eyebrow.

"No one," Brandon mumbles, glaring at Nico.

"Didn't look like no one to me, kid. You were making goo-goo eyes at her."

Brandon glares harder. "I wasn't."

"Shut up, Nico," Cash says and smiles at Brandon. "That's his study partner, right?" Cash asks, looking at Brandon.

Brandon's eyes narrow even further. "She's a friend," he grits out.

'Who's this?' I ask.

"She's no one. Just a friend from school," Brandon says.

"Friend… Hmmm," Trevor says.

Brandon glares at him. "She is a friend," he says.

Trevor gets a strange smile on his face. "Liz is my best friend," he says, which makes me chuckle.

"You're an idiot," Brandon says, laughing, and the rest of the guys laugh too.

"So, are we going to go fishing or sit around all day gossiping?" James asks, walking up to the group with his fishing pole.

"Come with me for a second, bud," I tell Brandon.

He follows me to the back of Asher's Jeep, where we have all our stuff stowed. When I open the hatch, I pull out the gift I got for him and hand it to him. His eyes go from me to the box then back again.

"What is it?" he asks.

"Open it," I tell him.

He pulls off the paper his mom insisted I wrap it in last night and his eyes go from his new pole to me.

"It's a good one,"

He swallows hard and nods.

"Your mom insisted on wrapping it even though I told her not to," I tell him.

His lips twitch and he looks at me again. "Thanks," he says.

I nod, patting him on the back. I fell in love with Kat a long time ago, but I have slowly fallen in love with her son over the last month.

"You want me to help you set it up?" I ask him.

He nods again, pulling it completely from the box. We spend the next ten minutes getting his new trigger pole ready to use. Once it's completely set up, I grab my pole and the tackle box I brought and head out to the boat we launched into the water when we arrived at the lake.

Once we all get in the boat, we head out into the middle of the lake, where the water is deeper and the fish radar is showing a school of fish below. We all cast off into the water and settle in for the day.

My dad used to bring my brother and me to this same lake when I was growing up. Most of our summers were spent out on the water. I have a lot of good memories here, and it feels good to share this place with Brandon. It makes me feel closer to him.

"I think you got something, bud," I tell Brandon as I watch the end of his pole bend slightly.

"How do you know?" he asks, looking from the pole to me.

"Watch the point of your pole," I tell him, and his eyes move to the pole. The end moves again.

"What do I do?" he asks quietly.

I look around the boat and see that everyone is focused on

Brandon and me. "You're gonna give your pole a tug. If something is on there, you want to make sure that it's hooked good and tight. Then you're gonna start reeling it in," I tell him.

He nods then does as I said, giving the pole a firm tug before reeling in the line.

"It's heavy," he says, his body and arms flexing as he fights against the fish that is determined to get away.

"You can do it," I tell him, standing at his side, coaching him the whole time—letting him know when to release some and when to bring the line in.

It takes a good half hour to get the fish to the top, and I'm surprised to see a giant bass break the surface of the water.

"Holy shit," Asher says, leaning over the side of the boat.

"That's one big fish!" Nico laughs and Brandon smiles looking over at me.

"Get the net," Cash tells Trevor.

"You did good, Kid," Trevor tells Brandon, leaning into the water to help Asher scoop out the fish.

"Well, you caught dinner," James says.

The smile that was on Brandon's face disappears in an instant. "You mean we're going to eat it?"

"Hell yes, we're going to eat it!" Asher smiles bringing the fish onto the boat.

"I never agreed to eating fish. Didn't we bring hot dogs or something?" Brandon asks, making me laugh.

"This is like the Wild West, Kid. You live off what you catch," Trevor tells Brandon, and all the boys laugh when Brandon shudders.

"You did good, bud," I say, bringing Brandon's attention to me. "I'm proud of you."

"It was cool," he says. Then he looks back at the fish then to me again. "Are you sure we don't have hot dogs?"

"I may have a pack in the cooler," I tell him, squeezing his shoulder.

"Thank God," he mumbles under his breath, making James and me laugh.

"SO, WHAT COLLEGE are you going to?" Cash asks Brandon. We just finished dinner and are now all sitting around the bonfire.

"I'm not sure. I may stay local and just do some business classes," Brandon tells him then looks over at me. "Joe said that, if I worked hard and proved to you both, he would talk to you about me managing Teasers."

"Did he?" I say. It doesn't surprise me that my brother would say something like that. I know he has been thinking about stepping back from the club just like I have.

"Well, he said that you guys are old," Brandon says with a smile, making me smile into the beer I just brought to my mouth.

"Didn't you just turn eighteen?" Cash asks, and Brandon nods. "You think you can run a strip club?"

"I don't think I can. I know I can," Brandon says, and pride fills my chest.

"You're a kid," Nico says.

"That doesn't mean anything."

"It does when there are naked women around," Trevor says.

"So, are you tryin' to say that Mike sleeps with the women who work at the club?" Brandon asks. "Or that Joe does?"

"I didn't say that," Trevor says, looking at me.

"Well, then, why would you think that I would do that?"

"You just turned eighteen," Cash repeats.

"And?"

"I think he could do it," I say.

All eyes come to me.

"Look at it this way. Joe and I opened teasers when we were in our twenties. I have never slept with or even touched one of the women who work for me nor do I want to. It's a job and nothing more. I think that, if he went to school, got some business classes or management classes under his belt, he could do good by the club and the girls. I know that he is young, but if he continues down the road he is on now, he will do amazing things one day," I say and turn to look at Brandon. "If you prove to me and Joe that you really want to run the club one day, I would be honored to hand the reins over to you."

I watch as his eyes go soft and a look I often see from his mom appears on his face before he looks away. I now know that I will do anything in my power to make sure he succeeds in whatever he chooses for his life and fully understands what my mom said to me when I told her that I wanted to own a strip club.

"All I have ever wanted was for you to be happy, son. So if this is what makes you happy and is a reason for you to get out of bed every day, then who am I judge it?"

From that moment on, my mom was my biggest ally, and I know that I will be that for Brandon.

"Thanks," Brandon says quietly.

"HOW DO YOU think Brandon would feel about you guys living with me?" I ask Kat.

We have been going strong for a few months. Most mornings,

when I get off work, I just come straight to Kat's. Even if I'm just going to be sleeping, I like knowing that Kat is in the next room. I can't stand being away from her. The idea of her moving in with me has been floating around in my head for some time now. Her townhouse is nice, but my house is nicer. I also have more space. Brandon wouldn't feel like we are living on top of him like he does now. I remember what it's like to be a teenage boy, and no way would I want my mom's room next to mine.

"You want us to move in with you?" Kat asks, her already large eyes getting larger.

"We basically live together now. I just figured we should make it official." I shrug like it's not a big deal even though my gut is twisting and my heart rate has sped up.

"Are you sure you want that?"

"Yes," I say immediately.

This is the next step for us. At this point, we're just putting off the inevitable. We spend all of our free time together and I never go home to my place anymore when I get off work unless there is something I need to do.

"I…" She pauses, looking around her place. "I wouldn't feel good about moving Brandon. Not right now in the middle of the school year."

Shit. I didn't even think about that. "Okay, so we wait and I'll move in here until the school year's done."

"You would do that?"

"Living with you isn't a hardship." I smile, crowding her against the counter in the kitchen. "Sleeping next to you." I nip her neck. "Waking up with you." I kiss her lips.

"So then, I guess we just need to sit down and talk to Brandon about it?" she whispers against my lips.

"You want both of us to talk to him or do you want to do it on your own?"

"I think I should talk to him first," she mumbles, looking down at her fingers that are now playing with the buttons of my shirt.

"Are you worried?" I ask, tilting her head back so I can see her eyes.

"No. I mean… I don't know." She shrugs. "He's been so good lately that I'm nervous about messing that up."

"Look, if we have to keep things the way they are right now, I'm cool with that."

She nods, and I kiss her on the mouth just as the front door is opens.

"Mom, Mike, I'm home!" Brandon yells.

"I'm gonna head home and you call me when you're done talking with him," I tell her, kissing her once more.

"Hey," Brandon says when he walks into the kitchen. His eyes go from his mom to me then back again.

"How was school?" Kat asks him as he opens the fridge door.

"School," he mumbles, pulling up his pants.

I don't even understand why he's wearing a belt when his pants are hanging off his ass anyways. I look at Kat, who blows out a long breath, looking at her son.

"I'm gonna head out," I say.

Kat pulls her eyes from Brandon's back before looking at me. "I'll walk you to the door."

"See you soon," I tell Brandon. I know he is supposed to be meeting me at the club in a few hours. Joe has some questions for him and wants to have a sit-down.

"I'm just gonna grab some food then change. I'll see you in a while," he mutters, not pulling his head from the fridge.

Kat squeezes my hand, and I follow her out of the kitchen to the front door.

"Call if you need me." I lean in and kiss her forehead then lips.

She nods when I pull away, and I can tell she's worried about talking to him about us.

"Look, if he's not okay with us moving in together, I'm cool with that."

"Who's moving in?" Brandon says from behind us.

Kat whispers, "Shit," under her breath before turning her head to look over her shoulder.

"If Mike's moving in, then I want to move to his house."

"What?" Kat asks, looking at him.

"His place is bigger." He shrugs. "Can I have the downstairs apartment?" he asks, taking a drink of his Coke and looking at me.

"That's up to your mom," I say, looking at Kat.

"I… Well… I guess that's something we will have to talk about," Kat says, stunned.

"Okay," he mumbles before walking up the stairs. "I have to head out to meet Asher before going to the club. Is it okay if I use the car?" he asks from the top of the stairs.

"Sure, honey," Kat tells him then looks at me when he is out of sight. "Okay, so that was weird."

I put an arm around her waist and pull her closer to me. "Looks like you're moving in," I tell her.

She looks from where Brandon just disappeared to me. "We are." She smiles.

Chapter 7

KAT

"SO WHAT'S YOUR day like?" Mike asks, crawling into bed next to me.

I close up my computer then look over at him. "I'm going to shower. I have to go to the school to meet with Brandon's teachers. Then I have a doctor appointment at two," I tell him, smiling when he pulls me closer to him.

"Why do you have to go to the doctor?"

"Just a checkup." I shrug like it's no big deal.

I don't want to tell him that I'm going through menopause. I hate getting old or older. It's not something you want to admit is happening when it's happening, but I can no longer pretend like I'm not going through the change.

"You sure?" he asks.

"Yes, I'm sure," I say, laying my head on his chest so that he can't read my face and figure out that I'm lying.

"What about Brandon?" he asks after a few seconds.

"His guidance counselor wants to meet about college."

He nods then leans back looking up at the celling.

I continue. "I know that he is adamant about not wanting to go away for college, but I really want him to hear all the choices before making a decision.

"Want me to come with you?" he tilts my face back to look at me.

"No." I shake my head while fighting a smile. I love him so much, and knowing that he cares about my son only makes that love grow even deeper.

"If you change your mind, let me know. I'm going to sleep while you shower," he says sleepily.

As much as I want to lie in bed with him, I know that, if I stay, he won't sleep. Since we've moved in, it has been getting harder and harder for him to go to the club in the evenings, and when he gets home in the morning, it's hard for me to leave him in bed alone.

"Get some rest and I'll see you when I get home." I kiss his jaw then roll out of bed and hurry to the bathroom without looking at him. I know that, if I see him in bed, I won't be able to help climbing back in with him.

"YOU'RE PREGNANT, MISS Mullings," the doctor says, stepping back into the room.

I look at him then shake my head. "There has to be a mistake," I say, trying to see the papers he's holding. "I'm going through menopause," I say, feeling another hot flash as soon as I say the word.

"You're not. You're too young. Normally, women go though menopause in their early fifties."

"I'm too old to be pregnant."

"You're healthy. You're not overweight. You don't smoke. Your blood pressure and vitals are all perfect. You have nothing to worry about." He smiles. He obviously has no idea what he's talking about, because Mike is going to freak out. "You're approximately eleven weeks along. We will need to keep a closer eye on you, but I expect things to go well. We will do an internal ultrasound to make sure that everything looks right, but I'm guessing, with your hormone levels, that everything is fine."

"Okay," I mumble. I have no idea what else to say. My brain has shut down.

I stay silent though the procedure. Even when I hear the heartbeat and see the little baby on the screen, it still doesn't feel real. When everything is done and I have discussed with the doctor what I should expect, I'm still in a daze. Then I wait for him to fill my prescription for prenatal vitamins before following him out to the front desk, where I make another appointment.

After my meeting at Brandon's school, all I wanted was a large glass of wine—now, I wanted the whole bottle.

I shake my head and head out to my car. I have no idea how I'm going to tell Mike this news. Things have just settled with us. We're at a good place in our relationship. I know that he didn't want a relationship after what had happened with November's mother, but I didn't know if he ever thought about having more kids.

A million thoughts race through my mind and I feel my stomach bubble with anxiety when I pull up in front of the house and see Mike's car as well as his mom's. I sit in silence for a few minutes, working up the courage to go inside. When I finally make it up to the front door, the sound of a little girl laughing greats me from the other side, and I take a deep breath before walking inside.

"Hey, babe," Mike says when he spots me standing in the hall watching him. He's sitting on the floor in the living room wearing one of his many band tees with a pair of jeans. June is standing between his spread legs, holding on to his fingers. "How was everything?" he asks.

I look from June's sweet face to Mike's and take a deep breath. "It was good," I tell him.

His eyes draw together. "What happened?"

"Nothing," I say, smiling when his mom walks into the room.

"Hey, girly," Emma, Mike's mom, says, walking across the room to me.

I meet her in the middle and give her a hug. My parents both live in Oklahoma, so having Mike's mom here in town along with the Maysons has made being away from family much easier.

"Where's my boy at?" she asks as the front door opens and Brandon walks in.

"Gran," Brandon says, giving her a hug. Then his eyes go to the floor where June is.

The moment June sees him, she starts gurgling and bouncing. She and July both love Brandon, and he loves both the girls.

"June bug," he says, getting down on his knees and holding out his hands.

June has been trying to learn to walk for a few weeks now. The farthest she has gotten when I have been around is two steps before giving up and crawling.

"Come here," Brandon says, holding out his hands, and June immediately lets go of Mike's fingers and walks four steps to Brandon before falling into his arms. "You're getting so good," he says, standing with her in his arms.

She laughs, looking into his face.

"You sure you're okay, baby?" Mike asks, coming to stand

next to me.

I nod and lean into his side, and his mom smiles at us then looks at Brandon with June. She laughs when June grabs Brandon's hair and pulls his face closer so she can gnaw on his chin.

"He's really great with kids," Mike's mom says. Then she looks at me and smiles. "So, do you want to go shopping with me this weekend?"

I immediately shake my head no and start thinking of something I need to do this weekend. Shopping with Emma is like pulling teeth. I don't even know why she calls it shopping when we're never in the store for more than a few minutes. I think she was happier than anyone in the world when online shopping was invented.

"I think Susan needs my help this weekend getting ready for the Halloween party that they are putting on downtown," I answer.

"Good. I'll call and see if she and November would like to go with us to pick up some stuff in Nashville. Then we can head over to the local warehouse store and pick up the stuff for the Halloween party."

"Okay, that would be nice," I tell her and feel Mike's body shaking behind me.

He knows that his daughter and I both hate shopping with his mom. November was actually the one to warn me about shopping with her grandma.

"I'm going to take June home before it gets too late," Emma says.

At the sound of her name, June turns her head in our direction, and when she sees me, she gets a huge smile on her face and holds out her hands towards me. I step away from Mike and take her from Brandon, and she immediately snuggles into my chest.

"Hi, June Bug," I say, rubbing my cheek over the top of her head.

The smell of her and feel of her in my arms causes me to tear up. Thinking about having this feeling while holding Mike's and my child in a few months is absolutely crazy. I lift my eyes and look at Mike—his eyes are pulled together like he's trying to figure something out. I smile and he smiles back, but I can still see the concern in his eyes.

"Are you going to come back for dinner?" I ask Emma.

She shakes her head no, running a hand over the top of June's head. "I have to go help November out tonight with the girls because Asher has some job he's working on and won't be home until late, and November is pregnant again, so Asher is on edge with leaving her alone."

"What?" I whisper in shock.

"Oh crap. There I go again, letting the cat out of the bag," she says, looking between Mike and me.

I can honestly say that I'm not even a little surprised that Asher and November are pregnant again. I know that they both wanted to have their children young and that Asher really wants a boy.

"Don't say anything until they announce it," Emma mumbles, walking over to the couch, where she grabs the diaper bag and June's sweater.

"Jesus," I hear Mike mumble.

Brandon laughs. I just stand there silently watching Emma gather all of June's belongings while trying to understand what I'm feeling. I will be pregnant at the same time that my boyfriend's daughter is pregnant. How in the world does that even happen? How awkward was it going to be when we both show up places at the same time?

"You okay, Mom?" Brandon asks.

I look at my son and do the only thing I can at this moment—I plaster a fake smile on my face. "Just great. So, what are you doing tonight?" I ask him.

He narrows his eyes but answers anyway. "I'm going to help a friend study for a test we have coming up in history."

"What friend is that?" I ask because he hasn't been hanging out with any of his old friends lately. If he's not working, he's at school or at home.

"Just a girl from class," he says.

Mike coughs behind me, so I swing my head to look at him before looking back at Brandon.

"A girlfriend?"

"A girl that is my friend, yes." He smiles.

"Should I be worried?"

He rolls his eyes at me. "No, Mom." He sighs.

"Will you be home for dinner?"

"No. I think were going to get something from the diner," he says and his cheeks brighten slightly, making me wonder who this girl is. "I have to go change. I'll be home by ten at the latest." He kisses the side June's head and then mine before disappearing downstairs to his room.

"Do you know who she is?" I ask Mike after a few moments.

"Nope, and if I did, I wouldn't tell you anyways."

"You wouldn't?" I ask, feeling my eyes narrow.

"Nope. Dude code, baby. We don't gossip with women about women."

"You don't gossip with women about women, but you gossip

about women to men?"

"Men don't gossip."

"Then what do you call it?"

"Exchanging valuable information."

"So…gossiping," I state.

"Nope." He smiles, leans in, and kisses me once.

"All right, June Bug. Come to Great-Grandma so Grandma and Grandpa can get some alone time," Emma says.

I almost blurt out, *"Holy shit!"* because I never thought that I was a grandma and I definitely never thought I would be a pregnant grandma. A grandma pregnant by a grandpa. Could my life get any more ridiculous?

"I'm gonna help Mom get her in the car," Mike says, so I kiss June one more time before passing her over to her grandfather.

"I will call and let you know what November and Susan say about our shopping trip," Emma says, following Mike out the door.

"Just let me know," I mutter, hoping that November is quick on her feet.

"Be back in a second," Mike says.

I watch him carry June to the car and put her in the car seat before kissing his mom's cheek and coming back up the stairs to me, where we both watch his mom drive away.

"Now will you tell me what's wrong?" Mike asks as soon as the front door is closed.

I turn to look at him. I want to tell him that I'm pregnant, but the words are stuck in the back of my throat.

"Nothing," I mumble and head for the kitchen, where I pull out the chicken breast I left to marinate in olive oil and a ranch dressing packet this morning.

"You don't seem like nothing's wrong," he says, watching me.

"I'm fine," I repeat as I start up the oven and place the chicken on a baking pan, before going into the pantry and getting a few potatoes to peel.

He comes over to where I'm standing at the sink and takes the potato peeler from my hand. Then he sets it on the counter next to the sink before turning me around to face him.

"What happened at the school?" he asks.

It takes a second for the question to register before I respond. "Nothing. Brandon has raised his GPA and the guidance counselor believes that he could get into pretty much any school he wants to," I tell him.

"Okay, so if it's not Brandon, then what happened at your appointment?"

"Nothing," I say then sigh when his eyes narrow. "Okay, promise you won't freak out."

"Kat."

"Just promise."

"Tell me," he says.

"I'm pregnant," I say when I realize that he's not going to give up or promise me that he won't freak out.

His body stills and his face goes blank immediately. "What?" he whispers so quietly that I more read his lips then hear the words.

"I'm pregnant," I repeat. I'm completely shocked that the words are coming out of my mouth.

I know a few women who waited until later in life to have children. I never thought that I would be having another child. I was sure that I wasn't even able to. When I was with my husband, we never used anything to prevent pregnancy. It just never happened. Plus, breast cancer runs in my family and my doctor advised against the pill.

"How did that happen?" Mike mumbles.

I close my eyes and drop my head. "Unprotected sex and stupidity," I answer, opening my eyes and looking at him.

His eyes roam over me then land on my stomach. "You're sure?"

I don't even say anything—I just walk to my bag, pull out the internal ultrasound pictures, and hand them to him.

"You're pregnant," he says, looking at the picture.

"I am."

"How far along are you?"

"He thinks eleven weeks," I say quietly, closely watching his face.

"Do you…" He stops to look at me and I see his Adam's apple bob as he swallows. "Do you want to keep it?"

Shit. Through all of this, I haven't even thought about not keeping him or her. I nod then bite my lip to keep from crying.

"Jesus, I don't even know what to say about this," he says, looking back down at the pictures.

"I don't know either."

"Will you be okay?" he asks, looking at me again.

"The doctor assured me that the baby and me should be fine."

"You're sure?"

"There are risks at my age, but he says they are minimal considering how healthy I am."

His body relaxes and his hands pull me closer as he shoves his face into my neck. "I'm scared to death but happy as hell," he says against my neck.

"Me too," I say, pushing my fingers through his hair.

"I think it's going to take a few days for this to sink in."

I smile as he kisses my neck before he pulls away and puts his hands on either side of my face.

"You're pregnant," he says, and I nod. "With my baby."

I smile and whisper, "Yes."

"Wow." He pulls my face towards his.

When I'm close enough, his lips press against mine. His tongue runs over my bottom lip and my mouth instinctively opens up under his. My hands fist into the front of his shirt so I can keep standing as his taste and the feel of his hands tangling into my hair cause my legs to go weak.

"You guys have a whole house. Do you have to do that in the middle of the kitchen?" Brandon says, breaking the moment.

Mike pulls his mouth from mine then smiles, looking over at Brandon. "Thought for sure that we would be on our own in a year. Looks like we have along ways to go until we have an empty house," Mike says quietly.

"What?" Brandon asks, walking fully into the kitchen. I notice that he's dressed in a nice sweeter and a pair of dark jeans that actually fit him.

"How do you feel about me marrying your mom?" Mike asks, and my stomach drops.

"What?" I whisper.

"I'm cool with it," Brandon says with a shrug.

"Do me a favor and run out to my car. There's a box in the glove box. Can you bring it to me?" Mike asks.

Brandon looks at me then Mike and heads towards the front door. I stand there, stunned, as Mike turns to face me.

"Give me one second, babe."

I don't say anything. I don't breathe or even blink as he heads towards the direction where Brandon just left. It feels like an eternity for them to come back. When they come back around the corner, Mike is holding a small box in his hand and Brandon is behind him with a large smile on his face.

"How do you feel about marrying me?" Mike asks, pulling my hand towards him and slipping the perfectly simple diamond ring on my finger.

"I had no idea," I stutter, looking at the ring on my finger. His laugh causes my head to come up and my eyes to meet his.

"I think that's the point, Kitten," he says softly as his hands come up to hold my face.

"You want to get married?" I ask him.

"Yes. I planned on asking you this weekend, but this seems like the perfect time to me," he says. Then he looks over at Brandon before looking back at me. "So what do you say? Will you and Brandon both take my last name?"

"What?"

"You and Brandon are mine and I would like it if we we're all Rouger's."

"I say yes," Brandon says, coming over to put his arm around my shoulder.

"Oh my God," I whisper, feeling a tear slide down my cheek.

"What do you say?" he asks again.

I tilt my head back to look at Brandon, who looks at me and nods, kissing the side of my head. "Yes," I say through my tears when my eyes meet Mike's again.

As soon as the word leaves my mouth, Mike's hands wrap into the back of my hair and his mouth crashes down onto mine.

"Can you guys control yourselves at least until I don't have to see it?" I hear Brandon say. I can tell by his tone that he's smiling.

I kiss Mike once more before whispering, "I love you," against his lips and then leaning back.

"Were you serious about us both having your last name?" Brandon asks after a minute.

"Yes," Mike replies, pulling me around to tuck me under his arm. "I would be honored if you had my last name."

Brandon swallows then looks at me. There are so many emotions in his eyes, and as his mom, I know that the look on his face is relief from being wanted and accepted. Without another word, Brandon wraps one arm around me then one around Mike. As I stand between my two guys, I burst into tears.

"Jeez, Mom. Relax." Brandon chuckles, and I feel Mike's laugher against my side.

"I'm fine. Just… Just happy." I cry, squeezing Brandon once more before stepping back.

"I know you have to go help your friend, but can you come home for dinner?" I ask and feel Mike's fingers squeeze into my side. I know that we just found out the news, but I really want my son to know what's going on.

"What's wrong?" Brandon asks.

"Nothing. Just come home for dinner," I sigh. Apparently, the men in my life don't know how to let up.

"Is this about Dad coming to visit?" he asks, his eyes drawn together.

"What?" Mike asks.

I double-blink. I haven't heard anything from my ex in over a month. He sent me an e-mail after I confronted him about canceling his designated time with Brandon that was scheduled for Thanksgiving. When I found out that he'd told Brandon that he couldn't come out for four days because his girlfriend's parents were in town and there was just no room, I flipped out. I was tired of him letting his son down and not caring about disappointing his child.

"What do you mean your dad is coming here?" I ask, confused.

Brandon shrugs. "I don't know. He sent me a text telling me he would be here next week after I told him that I wouldn't be coming out for any of my scheduled visitation times."

"Great," I whisper.

"I'm guessing that's not the reason you wanted me to be home."

"It's not." I shake my head.

"Just come home after your study date, bud, and we'll talk then," Mike says.

Brandon nods and pulls me in for another hug. "Love you, Mom," he says quietly.

I take a shuddering breath before telling him that I love him too and watching him leave. When I turn to face Mike, his eyes are so soft that my breath pauses.

"You have no idea how much you have done for not only me but for Brandon," I tell him, closing my eyes before opening them slowly. I know that Brandon and I would have been okay eventually, but I doubt that our relationship would have healed like it has without him.

"I haven't done anything, Kitten."

"You have. You have helped bring my son back to me. You have given him something he hasn't received from his dad since he was little and you have given that to him when he needs it most. So, yes, you have done a lot."

"It's not a hardship to love him. He's a good kid. And you're an amazing mom, and your ex… Well, he's a piece of shit." He smiles, walking towards me. "I figure we have a couple of hours before he comes home. What do you say we go upstairs and celebrate our engagement?" he says.

I look down at my hand and the ring that is sitting on my finger before bringing my eyes back up to meet his. "I think I like that idea," I tell him and start to laugh when he quickly pulls his shirt off over his head. I pause, checking out his body before pulling my shirt up over my head and turning towards the stairs. I hear his footsteps behind me and my pulse begins to speed up as wetness floods between my legs.

"Careful," he says against my ear as his hand slides around my waist.

Even though I know what's coming, I still have butterflies in my stomach. My pulse skids as his hand cups my pussy and his fingers press into the seam of my jeans.

"Oh," I hiss as my head falls back onto his shoulder.

He grunts something, but I can't make it out as his fingers move to the button of my jeans and his other hand slides up to cup my breast over my bra. When he has my jeans unzipped and his fingers slide between my folds, I moan and lift my hands over my head to grip into his hair.

"So slick," he says against my neck, and his fingers slide up and around my clit.

"I need you inside me," I hiss, feeling my pussy contract.

He removes his hand and places his fingers in his mouth before pulling my chin towards him and taking my mouth in a deep kiss. The taste of myself on his mouth has me grabbing, pulling at the buckle of his belt. When I almost have it undone, his hand covers mine.

"Bed," he demands, and my eyes go to his.

My knees almost buckle at the hunger I see in his eyes. I nod, and without another word, I rush up the stairs into the bedroom, listening as his footsteps follow me up the stairs. I turn around and face the door. As soon as I reach the bed, my hands go to behind my back and my fingers work quickly to unhook my bra. Once it's unclasped, I lean forward and let it drop off my shoulders and onto the floor. When my eyes meet his and he smirks, he is pushing his pants down over his hips. I lick my lips as I watch his cock bounce against his stomach. Then I strip of my jeans and panties, quickly kicking them to the side as I watch him stroke himself.

"Climb up on the bed and lay back, spreading your legs, Kitten," he demands.

I listen, getting up onto the bed and lying back. I sit up on my elbows, watching as he walks towards me, his eyes locked between my legs. I start to scoot back, expecting him to climb up on the bed, but his hand around my ankle stops me. He pulls me back towards the edge of the bed before lowering his face and sucking the skin of my inner thigh deep into his mouth, causing me to whimper and my back to rise off the bed.

"Hmmm," he breathes, licking up to the crease of my leg right on the edge of my pussy.

I wiggle my hips and grab his hair with one hand. I feel his smile against my skin and whimper as he pulls one pussy lip into his mouth, Then I feel the edge of his tongue slide near my entrance as his fingers dig into my thighs. He spreads my legs farther apart before his lips cover my clit and he pulls it into his mouth. I feel my orgasm building as his fingers fill me, moving slowly as he releases my clit and moves up my body. One arm holds me under my back as he lifts me onto the center of the bed. I pull his face down to mine, kissing him, tasting myself on his mouth. I lift my hips and wrap one leg around his hip as his fingers slide out and he enters me.

"God," I moan, feeling myself clamp down on him. I scrape my nails down his back as his hand cups my breast and his fingers tug on my nipple.

"Your pussy is so fucking hot," he growls against my mouth, and I moan into his, placing the heels of my feet into the back of his thighs so I can lift my hips to meet each of his thrusts with one of my own.

My hand travels up his back into his hair before sliding down his neck and over his shoulder and chest. Then I flip it to run over my stomach so my fingers can roll over my clit. He leans back and looks down, watching as I touch myself. His eyes get even darker as he slows his thrusts and sits up on his knees, his thumbs holding my pussy lips apart as he watches himself sink into me.

"I'm so close," I moan, rolling my fingers over my clit faster as his thrusts speed up. At this angle and with the way he's hitting my G-spot, my orgasm is building rapidly. When his hand pushes mine away and his finger rolls over my clit, my head digs into the pillow behind me.

"Pull those nipples, baby," he grunts, and I lift my hands to my breasts and pull my nipples as he pounds into me.

My orgasm is sudden and my body vibrates. White light fills my vision and I feel like I float away. I slowly come back to myself and feel him grow larger as his hips jerk and he groans, planting himself deep inside me. His body comes forward, covering mine while keeping his weight off my lower abdomen. I let out a long breath and run my hands up his back into his hair, listening closely as his breathing evens out.

"Every time I think about my kid inside you, I want to beat my chest," he says, making me laugh as he presses his face deeper into my neck. "Promise you won't leave me," he whispers after a couple of minutes.

I swallow against the lump in my throat and pull his face away from my neck so I can look into his eyes. "You're stuck with us. We're not going anywhere," I tell him and watch relief flash in his eyes before he lowers his mouth back to mine.

"SO ARE YOU going to tell me what's going on?" Brandon asks as we sit down for dinner.

I look at Mike, and he squeezes my thigh under the table. "You're going to be a brother," I tell him, deciding that I may as well just get it over with.

"What do you mean I'm going to be a brother?" he asks, confused.

I take another breath, thinking that this is much harder than it was when I told Mike. "I mean I'm pregnant."

"But you're old," he blurts, looking at Mike and then me.

"Hey, I'm not that old," I scold him.

Mike starts to laugh.

"Mom, you're not young. I'm eighteen. It's just weird that you're having a kid after so many years," he says.

"The doctor assures me that everything will be okay."

"It's still weird," he mumbles, taking a bite of the meatloaf I made for dinner. "I'm happy that my room is in the basement. I don't want a screaming kid to wake me up in the middle of the night," he says, not even looking up from his plate.

I look over at Mike, who shrugs and takes a bite of his dinner. I look at my two men then down at my stomach and let out a breath. Things are going to change drastically when the baby gets here. But I am happy that my two men are taking this whole thing so well.

Now we have to see what everyone else thinks about it.

Chapter 8

MIKE

"**C**AN YOU BELIEVE that he had the nerve to show up and make a spectacle like we were together? Like we're a couple?" Kat rambles as I pull up to the front of the house. "How could he be so stupid? I mean really, what the hell is wrong with him?"

I don't say anything. I can't after the last hour. My blood pressure still hasn't gone back to normal. I'm at a loss for words as to what just happened.

I've never thought that her ex was a smart man, but when he showed up at Brandon's school, pulled Kat to him, and kissed her, I lost my shit. I'd known that he was coming to town, but what I hadn't known was his reasoning. Apparently, he broke up with his girlfriend and thought that he was coming back to claim his wife. The fuck now has two black eyes to prove that he isn't getting anywhere near my woman—ever.

"I hate him. I hated him before, but now, I really, really hate him. I hope…" She pauses to take a breath. "I hope he gets run over by a bus. Too bad we don't have buses in town," she mutters under her breath as I shut off the car and hop out.

After walking around to her side to help her out, I take her hand and help her up the stairs and into the house.

"Really, who does he think he is?" she asks before rambling some more while pulling off her cap and unwrapping the scarf she had tied around her neck.

I walk straight into the kitchen, open the cupboard above the fridge, and pull down my whiskey before pulling the cap off and putting the bottle to my lips to take a swig.

"That's really not fair," Kat states as I put the bottle down on the counter.

"Sorry, Kitten," I say and put the lid back on the bottle. "Come here," I tell her, feeling the liquid heat of the alcohol lessening some of the anger I'm feeling.

She looks at me for a few seconds before walking to where I'm standing. When she's close enough, I wrap my arms around her.

"How are you feeling?" I ask, rubbing her back.

"Pissed."

"I got that, Kitten. How's our boy?"

"He's fine," she says and immediately melts into me.

Earlier in the week, we found out that we would be adding another boy to our family. Everyone was overjoyed. Well, everyone except Asher, who had found out the week before that he and my baby girl were going to be adding another girl to their bunch. When we told everyone that we were expecting, they were all really excited about the news, and November was more than excited about becoming a big sister—even if she already considered Brandon her brother.

"Do you think Brandon will be okay?"

"He's fine." I rub her back again. "He said he was going to talk with his dad and then he would be home," I remind her.

Brandon was upset with his father as well but had tried to

neutralize the situation and agreed to go talk with his dad while I took Kat home. I was proud of him.

"I can't believe you punched him." She pauses then looks up at me and smiles. "Twice."

"He had his hands and mouth on you," I growl, my anger returning at the memory. "He's lucky that he was able to walk away and that Trevor was there to hold me back after I got the first two hits in."

I never thought that, at my age, I would be fighting at a high school function. But seeing that fuck touch my woman—the woman carrying my child—had my blood boiling.

I hear Kat's yawn and look down at her, realizing that she has been going all day. The stress of this situation added on top of her pregnancy has her worn out.

"Head up and get ready for bed, babe. I'm going to send Brandon a message to make sure he's okay before locking up."

"Okay." She yawns again, and I kiss her forehead and pat her bottom. "I'll meet you in bed," she says, walking away.

When I hear the water turn on upstairs, I send I message to Brandon asking if he's okay. I quickly get a reply that let me know that he just got in his car and is on his way home. I clean up the kitchen and wait until I hear Brandon pull up outside. Then I open the front door and meet him on the porch.

When I see him, I can tell that he is stressed. As much as he has matured over the last few months, he is still a young kid, and sometimes, it's hard to remember that.

"You okay?" I ask him, letting him inside.

"Yeah. He's heading home tomorrow. I guess the only reason he wanted to come was to see if he had a chance of getting back with Mom," he says.

I want to get in my car, head to the fuckwad's hotel, and beat the shit out of him for hurting his kid *again*.

"Sorry, bud," I tell him, squeezing his shoulder.

"Nothing with him surprises me anymore."

"You wanna talk about it?"

"Nah. I want to go to bed. Can you tell Mom I said good-night?"

"Sure," I tell him, watching as he heads down the basement stairs.

I finish locking up and set the house alarm before heading upstairs. When I reach the bedroom, Kat is already asleep, so I make quick work of my clothes before getting into bed behind her and pulling her into me.

"Is Brandon home?" she asks sleepily when I kiss the back of her head.

"Yeah," I tell her, running my hand over her slightly rounded stomach.

"I should go make sure he's okay."

"He went to bed and said to tell you goodnight." I whisper.

"I hate that he has to go through this."

"Me too, Kitten." I sigh, tucking her closer to me.

I wish there were something I could do for both her and Brandon, but I know that this situation is beyond my control. Kat, her ex, and Brandon will be tied together for the rest of their lives whether I like it or not. The only thing I can do I is be here for both of them when they need me.

I wait and listen for Kat's breath to even out before closing my eyes and following her off to sleep.

I WALK INTO the kitchen and stop when my eyes land on Kat and Brandon. They are leaning on the counter and have their heads together, looking at some recipe book. I watch as Kat says something, making him laugh, then bumps him with her hip, smiling at him. I like knowing that our son is going to have this, that he is going to grow up with people around him who want and love him and that he will never feel like November felt growing up.

"Let's go pick out a Christmas tree," I say after a few more seconds of watching them.

Both her and Brandon's heads rise at the same time, and Kats eyes draw together in confusion.

"It's not even Thanksgiving," she says, standing up. I smile when I see the small bump that is starting to form on her stomach.

"I know, but it's a tradition I started when November moved home. I always get her a tree. And now that we're a family, I would like to get one for us as well so that we can start our own traditions," I say, looking at first Brandon then down at Kat's stomach.

I missed out on so much with November; I refuse to miss out on anything now.

I still couldn't believe that I was going to be a dad and that I would be having a son. I had given up hope of having a larger family a long time ago. I never would have dreamed that I would be getting married or having a baby or marrying a woman who had a child already and adopting him as my own. Life has a way of giving you everything you didn't even know you needed, and Kat, Brandon, and now our new little one are proof of that.

"Do we need to buy Christmas decorations?" Kat asks.

Brandon groans behind her. Kat loves to shop and could

spend hours in one store just walking around.

"We can do that another time," I say.

Brandon mumbles, "Thank God," under his breath, making me laugh and causing Kat to roll her eyes.

When we get to the tree farm, we spend way more time than is necessary looking at trees. When I was on my own, I would come here and pick out whatever tree was closest to the entrance of the farm. But like she does when she's shopping, Kat has to look at and compare each tree before settling on one. I swear she does it to be a pain in the ass. She liked two trees when we got to the farm but insisted on looking around only to end up coming back to the first two.

"That wasn't so bad," Kat says with a smile, sipping on her hot chocolate.

"Mom, you had us walk around for over an hour only to come back to the first trees you saw," Brandon says.

"I wanted to make sure we got good ones," she says then looks at me.

I can't help but laugh at the innocent look on her face. "Let's get these tied down, bud," I tell Brandon when I see that he is going to say something else.

I send a message to Asher to make sure he and November are home before getting back into the truck with Kat pressed to my side and Brandon sitting next to the door. As soon as we pull up in front of November's house, July and June are on the porch, jumping up and down, while November stands behind them with a smile on her face. I get out and help Kat, walking her up the front steps, where she and November hug and start laughing when the girls yell, "*Uncle Brandon,*" and attack him before he even makes it up all the steps. Once he has both girls picked up, one on each side of him, he makes it up the rest of the steps, the girls talking to him about God knows what.

"Hi, Daddy," November says, smiling at me.

"Hey, baby girl," I say and pull her in for a hug before releasing her and putting my arm around Kat's shoulder.

"Tree time already?" Asher asks with a smile.

"Yep," I tell him.

He nods then kisses November's head before heading down the stairs to the truck. I kiss Kat and Brandon puts the girls down before we follow behind Asher and work at getting the tree inside.

Chapter 9

KAT

"**I**T'S CHRISTMAS ALREADY?" July asks, looking at me then her mom.

"No, baby." November laughs. "Grandpa always brings me a tree before my birthday and Thanksgiving," she explains.

"Oh." July pouts. "When do we get presents from Santa?" she asks, making me laugh.

"On Christmas, but you have to be good."

"I'm good. June's not always good," she says, lifting her chin.

November bites her lip and looks at me then back down at July, who is watching the men put up the tree. "Is tattling being good?" she asks July.

"I didn't twattle," she says, her eyes going wide.

"Just making sure." November laughs.

July jumps off her lap and runs to her dad, pouting out her lip. I can't hear exactly what he says, but I can tell by the look on her face that it must make it better.

"Dad's so happy," November says quietly.

I look at her then over at Mike, who turns his head and winks when his eyes meet mine.

"I wanted him to find someone. I set him up on an online

dating website and pushed him to date, but he was never really into it. I thought that he would spend the rest of his life alone. I never would have thought that he would be getting married and having a baby. And that I would be getting not only one but two brothers." She smiles and lets out a small laugh.

"I never expected all of this either," I say quietly, laying my hand against my stomach.

"Well, I'm excited. Even if Asher is jealous that you're having a boy," she says, and I laugh. "He swears he's cursed with girls because he was a man-whore." She rolls her eyes, and I laugh harder.

"What are you guys talking about?" Asher asks.

I immediately stop laughing, look at November, and feel my eyes go wide.

"Oh, nothing," November tells him, leaning back in her chair so she can smile up at him.

"Hmmm," he grunts then bends down and kisses her. "I'm going to head up to the attic and get the Christmas decorations. The girls want to decorate tonight," he says.

November sighs. "Honey, it's late. They need to take a bath."

"Babe…" is all he says, and she shakes her head.

"Okay, honey," she mumbles. When he walks away, she says, "When our girls get older, he is so screwed."

"Tired?" Mike asks.

I roll over to look at him. "Yes, but I had a really great time," I tell him, wrapping my arm around his stomach. "June and July have their daddy wrapped around their little fingers." I smile.

"They do," he agrees and takes a breath. "I couldn't ask for more for my daughter or my grandbabies. He loves all of them unconditionally and would do anything for them."

"I love that for them," I say, kissing his chest.

"Just think. Next year, that will be us and our little man," he says, and I smile.

"I can't wait to make thousands of memories with you," I tell him quietly.

"Me too, babe," he says, kissing the top of my forehead.

After seeing Mike with his granddaughters and Brandon, I know that the memories we make as a family will be extra special.

Epilogue

MIKE

A few years later

"So, you're going to let me run the club?" Brandon asks.

I nod. I never really thought about retiring at my age, but I like the idea of being home with Kat. Brandon has taken it upon himself to get management classes under his belt, and he had also proven himself mature enough on more than one occasion to run the club without me around. I knew that he would take the job seriously and always treat the girls at the club with respect. He also works well with Joe, and that says a lot. My brother is difficult and doesn't trust many people, but he loves Brandon like his own kid.

"Yep. I'm handing the reins over to you. But if you need me, I'll be around," I tell him, watching as his face changes.

He looks away from me and scrubs his hands down his face before lowering his head, his shoulders slumping. "I know you're not my dad," he says, and I can hear the strain in his voice.

"I'm not," I tell him, watching as he slowly lifts his head.

"You're not my dad, but you're the man I look up to. The man who has shown me how to be a man, and for that, I will always be grateful and would be honored if you would let me call you Dad."

I sit back in my chair and look at the man in front of me. The kid who used to wear jeans that were way too baggy now wears suits on a daily basis. His hair, which was shaggy, is now groomed and cut into a style that says he cares about his appearance. Women and men notice him when he walks into a room. Where he used to be quick to anger, he is now cautious in his reactions. I didn't raise him, but he is no longer the boy I once knew. He is now a man, and I would like to think I had something to do with that.

"I would be proud to call you my son," I tell him.

I watch his eyes fill with tears. Then he takes a breath and shakes his head smiling.

"I'm not gonna cry about this shit." He shakes his head again before standing up. "I have work to do. Can you tell Mom that I'll see her this weekend for Christmas dinner?"

"Of course," I mutter, my chest still compressed from the sheer weight of what just happened. "You bringing a date?" I ask when he gets to the door.

"No, Dad, and you can tell Mom I said that," he says before walking out the door and shutting it behind him.

I take a deep breath, letting it out slowly. Then I pick up the phone, call Kat, and tell her that I will be home for dinner.

ASHER

"BABY, WAKE UP. It's Christmas," I whisper to November, who grunts and rolls away from me. Nothing much has changed since we got together. "Baby, we need to get up. Everyone's gonna be here soon."

"Go away," she mutters, sticking her head under the pillow.

"Baby, we gotta make breakfast," I remind her.

"Asher, I swear I will kill you one of these days," she cries, making me chuckle.

I force her to her back before placing my mouth over hers in a deep kiss. Then I lift her out of the bed and put her on her feet.

"Now go get ready to help me make breakfast," I say before smacking her ass and leaving the room.

TREVOR

"STAY LIKE THAT," I groan into Liz's ear and plant myself balls-deep inside her tight pussy. I swear I will never get enough of this, of her.

"Don't stop. Please. I'm so close," she whispers, and I smile and slide back out.

"Not gonna stop, babe. Just hold still," I tell her again, swiveling my hips.

"Yesss," she hisses.

"Dada, frewnd!" I hear my son cry.

I stop and look down at Liz, who narrows her eyes on me.

"It's Christmas!" my daughter yells through the baby monitor in my son's room. Then my boy starts to laugh.

I lay my head against Liz's back and want to cry—my kids are total cock blockers.

"You owe me ten orgasms," Liz says, falling to her stomach. "And hours of oral," she adds, putting her head under the pillow.

"Sorry, baby. Merry Christmas," I tell her, kissing her quickly and getting out of bed to go get my kids.

CASH

"WHAT THE HELL?" I put out my hand in search of Lilly and come up with a small, cloth-covered foot. I lift my head, look across the expanse of our California king bed, and see that Jax and Ashlyn have both gotten into bed with us and are lying crossways in the bed between Lilly and me. I sit up and straighten first Jax then Ashlyn before making my way over to Lilly. Lying down along her back and wrapping my arms around her, I breathe in her scent.

"It's Christmas," she whispers.

I smile against her neck. "It is. Do you want your gift?" I ask, rubbing myself against her.

"Nice try, mister. I know the kids are in bed with us," she groans.

"They are. I guess you'll have to get my gift later," I tell her, kissing her neck and making her laugh.

"Daddy, it's Christmas!" I hear behind me.

I roll to my back just in time for Ashlyn to land on my gut, making me grunt.

"Do we get to open owe pwesents now?" Jax asks.

I look over at Lilly as Ashlyn crawls on top of her and Jax comes to lie on my chest.

"First, you have to brush your teeth. Then you can see what Santa brought for you," Lilly says.

At that, both the kids get out of bed and take off out of the room.

"Alone at last," Lilly says, running her fingers through my hair as I lower my mouth to hers.

"Santa came!" the kids shout.

I groan, closing my eyes. "We need another 'naked house'

day," I tell her, and she smiles.

"Well, then, I guess I got you the perfect gift," she says, getting out of bed.

I watch her go before lying back, looking up at the ceiling, and smiling.

NICO

"I CAN'T FIT into anything!" Sophie cries lying back on the bed in a huff. Her large, pregnant stomach rolls as our daughters move around. Her naked breasts rise and fall and her pussy is slightly visible through the thin, white fabric she's wearing.

"You looked good in what you had on," I tell her, kneeling down between her legs with my hands on her stomach.

Her head comes up and she looks at me, her cheeks flushed and her eyes narrow. "I look like a whale," she says, laying her head back down. "A giant, stuffed whale."

"You look gorgeous, sexy as fuck," I tell her and pull down her panties, tossing them behind me. "You look good enough to eat." I breathe over her pussy, which is pink and swollen from pregnancy.

"Nico," she whimpers, raising her hips.

My beautiful girl is so sensitive; the slightest touch is enough to set her off lately. I love her pregnant. Her body is so ripe. Her taste is fucking addictive.

"Breathe, baby," I say against the lips of her sex before spreading them open with my thumbs and taking a swipe of her with my tongue. The second her taste fills my mouth, I go at her, burying my face in her pussy.

"Best. Christmas. Gift. Ever," she whispers.

I couldn't agree more.

MIKE

I LOOK AROUND the table at everyone. James has his arm around Susan. Asher has his hand on November's stomach as he and May talk to her four-months-pregnant stomach. Trevor has Liz and his son on his lap. Cash and Lilly are locked in their own private moment while Nico is whispering something to Sophie that is making her smile.

I feel a hand on my thigh, and when I look to my right, my eyes meet Kat's soft ones. I lean over and place a kiss on her lips. When my son yells, I watch as he holds out the turkey thigh he was eating to Beast, laughing when Beast licks it. I take a full breath then look at Brandon, who looks at me and smiles before laughing at something the kids are doing.

I'm always thankful for what I have, but this year, I'm thankful for the second chances I didn't even know were possible to have.

Other books by this Author

The Until Series
Until November

Until Trevor

Until Lilly

Until Nico

Underground Kings Series
Assumption

Obligation – Coming Soon

Distraction – Coming Soon

Alpha Law
Justified – Coming Soon

Liability – Coming Soon

Verdict – Coming Soon

Acknowledgment

First I want to give thanks to God without him none of this would be possible.

Second I want to thank my husband for always being so supportive and cheering me on even when I want to throw in the towel. To my editor Missy thank you for helping me to enjoy the story of Mike and Kat and thank you Mickey for all your hard work and your amazing brain. Thank you to my cover designer and friend—*I don't care if she thinks we're friends or not cause in my head we are*, Sara Eirew your design skills are unbelievable and I will shout that from the rooftops.

Thank you to TRSOR you girls are always so hard working I will forever be thankful for everything you do. To my Beta's I think I have said it a million time's but I couldn't ask for better, thank you all so much for pushing me to finish this book even when you basically had to beat me into it. Aurora's Roses I wish I could hug each and every one of you. I wish you could all know how much you all brighten my days. To every Blog and reader thank you for taking the time to read and share my books. And to my FBGM girls I'm always grateful to be on this journey with each of you.

XOXO
Aurora

About the Author

Aurora Rose Reynolds is a navy brat whose husband served in the United States Navy. She has lived all over the country but now resides in Tennessee with her husband and their Great Dane Blue. She's married to an alpha male that loves her as much as the men in her books love their women. He gives her over the top inspiration every day. Last but not least she is grateful for everyday.

For more information on books that are in the works or just to say hello, follow me on Facebook:
www.facebook.com/pages/Aurora-Rose-Reynolds/474845965932269

Or Goodreads
www.goodreads.com/author/show/7215619.Aurora_Rose_Reynolds

Or Twitter
@Auroraroser

Or E-mail Aurora she would love to hear from you
Auroraroser@gmail.com

And don't forget to stop by her website to find out about new releases.
AuroraRoseReynolds.com

CPSIA information can be obtained
at www.ICGtesting.com
Printed in the USA
LVHW05s1813170618
581007LV00044B/3065/P